# Circus of Horrors

# Circus of Horrors

*Carole Gill*

Copyright (C) 2015 Carole Gill
Layout Copyright (C) 2016 Creativia

Published 2016 by Creativia
Paperback design by Creativia (www.creativia.org)
ISBN: 978-1530653898
Cover art by http://www.thecovercollection.com/
This book is a work of fiction. Names, characters, places, and incidents are the product of the author's imagination or are used fictitiously. Any resemblance to actual events, locales, or persons, living or dead, is purely coincidental.
All rights reserved. No part of this book may be reproduced or transmitted in any form or by any means, electronic or mechanical, including photocopying, recording, or by any information storage and retrieval system, without the author's permission.

# Chapter 1

The vehicle was a beat up well-travelled 1929 Ford school bus. It had been painted a bright red and said 'Fred Dodger's Circus' on the side. Amid peeling paint, the image of ecstatic clowns was a bit pathetic looking. Curtains hung on each of the windows. Baby Alice had sewn them; now she sat outside with her pals waiting for the meat to be cooked.

An old man, somewhat senile in appearance and actions, sat licking his lips. His son, the owner/manager, had gone to town on business in his pickup.

The bus had withstood a lot of wear and tear. Well, it would have—what with three clowns, two midgets, and one fat lady riding it.

Al drove the bus. With him being three feet tall, there were adaptions to the driver's seat. This, the manager had seen to and Al was pleased. His lady friend, the huge Baby Alice, sat near him. Her seat had also been adapted in order to accommodate her girth.

None of the troupe disliked riding in the bus or camping out in tents. The weather occasionally made it difficult for them, though. Once, near Tupelo, Mississippi, the bus had to be dragged out by the pickup. The manager had extensive experience in such matters and everyone was grateful he did.

Fred Dodger loved his people and looked after them very well, and they knew it. He had explained about leaving them to go to town in order to get some money. They said fine and decided to have a cook out.

Any car or truck driving past would have been amused at the scene. Clearly, they were circus people—carnies—with the clowns in full make-up, Alice who weighed just under two hundred and fifty pounds, and Hank and Al, both three feet tall.

Hank got to arguing with Al about the progress of the meat being cooked. When it was at last ready, Al served it up. The old man got his first out of respect. He dug right in. Baby Alice did the same, as did the clowns. Al and Hank had a salami they swiped from a deli. They weren't going to eat what everyone else was eating. They weren't cannibals.

They spoke while they chewed their salami. "I have to hand it to you," Al said. "It makes for a perfect solution—cooking them guys the way you did."

Hank agreed. "Three sailors, think of it!"

"They deserved it. Didn't deserve no better!"

"True, but there *were* three of them. We're just lucky we didn't have far to take them."

"Yeah, imagine them snooping close to us. I wonder what Fred would have done."

"He wouldn't have liked their taunts."

The sailors had insulted everyone. Baby Alice was reduced to tears and the old man had been pushed when he objected to their language. Then they started in on the boys. Yes, boys—despite being 38 and 40, Al and Hank thought of themselves as that: kids, in trouble. The popular Katzenjammer Kids comic duo had nothing on them.

The boys didn't take shit from anyone. What were three more big mouthed louts to them? Al whipped out his razor. The dispute was settled in five bloody minutes. Where the sailors had been nasty fools taunting those they saw as misfits, they soon became blood-drenched corpses, their throats cut so deep, their heads dangled.

"Good thing the boss ain't here."

Al agreed. He knew they owed a lot to the clowns.

The clowns took care of everything—they cut them up into manageable parts, then basted them with some Heinz sauce, their favorite.

It took all day for the meat to be ready. When they could finally taste it, the clowns were proud and Baby Alice said it was the best she'd had in a long time. Hank made lemonade. It was luxurious, sitting out in the early dusk of a cool June evening.

\* \* \*

Most of the meat had been eaten when Fred came back. "Smells good. Any left for me?"

The boys looked at one another. Fred nodded toward his father who was still chomping away on what looked like a couple of fingers. When he walked toward the man, the boys started to worry big time. Snatching a thumb out of his hand, Fred shouted, "Christ Almighty! I warned you guys!"

He had and more than once. Al started to explain about the sailors, but Fred was having none of it. "I don't like my father eating human flesh! That's my main gripe. Okay?"

The boys nodded. "It won't happen again." They looked sincere. Fred doubted that they were. "Just don't let me see you do it again."

Total hypocrisy, but Fred did feel sorry for them.

Old Pa had begun to doze. "Come along; time to turn in, old 'un."

The old man found it hard to stand. His joints cracked and he shook his head. "These old bones," he said as the half eaten thumb fell to the ground. Alice glanced at it and giggled.

Fred led his dad toward the pickup. No tent for Old Pa. Not at his age. Fred had a nice, cozy, little box-like enclosure he constructed himself for them both to sleep in, in the pickup.

"I got it all accomplished in town, Dad. Got them checks cashed. We should be fine for a while."

The old man nodded. "I'm tired out..."

"I know. That's why you're going to be sleeping in a sec!"

His people watched them go. They liked being with Fred and his father. It was like having a family. Better really, considering how they were raised.

Al and Hank grew up in orphan asylums—graduating eventually to mental hospitals. Baby Alice lived with her father who beat her. She ran away to live with a succession of men who did the same. Her best day came when she started to work freak shows as the fat lady. People were nuts, fucked up in one way or another. She made extra money on the side for those patrons that wanted a flash—a buck to flash her naked, oversized jugs and a buck fifty for a feel. If they wanted more, and some of them did, the price went as high as five dollars. That hadn't happened since Fred hired her.

Besides, she had a boyfriend now. She and Al were a couple. How the two managed it, Fred had no idea, but from the look on Al's face, he was sure something had been figured out. Over time, a relationship had grown between the two of them. Which was nice, Fred thought. It would keep them both on the straight and narrow.

After tucking the old man in, Fred emerged and gave the clowns an angry stare. "I don't like the cannibalism. I don't like it at all."

The clowns started to argue with him. Happy was the most vociferous. Before the old man went senile, he used to ask him why he let the clowns join up. Fred would reply he felt sorry for them. How do you not pity feel sorry for three men who hide behind garish clown makeup because they know it's less frightening for people than their own faces?

Each had been cut up and scarred when they were little. They came from an orphanage where they were burned with cigarettes and cut up with razor blades, leaving their faces in horrific condition. They got the idea of the clown makeup from an old carny they had befriended. He taught them how to be clowns and showed them how to cover their scars up. When he applied the cooling pancake, they giggled. Jocko had been their friend until he died. It was through him they discovered the carny life.

"I think we pissed him off," Noble said, meaning Fred.

"Can't please everybody." Danny shrugged.

"What am I going to do with you guys?"

"Love us?" Happy offered.

# Chapter 2

Fred was pleased to hear Old Pa snoring. He had fallen asleep in an instant. He had his usual pee in the pot kept for such purposes and was now away with the fairies. Fred smiled. He had loved that expression as a child.

He began thinking of his people. They didn't mind life on the road, the tents or anything. They were used to a lot worse. He pitied each one of them. What a strange group they were.

His dad, Charlie, had only been in a few sideshows back in England. He didn't have what it took, though. He'd tried clowning and juggling—managing too when given a few chances, but none of it worked. Charlie wasn't the circus type.

He did stay with the clowning but there were reasons for that. He liked being anonymous. And he liked making kids laugh. He was a great dad despite his troubled past. Fred could remember how Old Pa had been the only good thing in his life.

"I'm all you got, lad. Sorry."

Fred could barely remember his mother, which was just as well. He had loved her, he knew that, but then she died and he didn't like to think of it.

His dad had a rough time raising him. It couldn't have been easy.

They lived in a lot of places; London, mainly, although there were many other places they called home for a while. But, London was the place he remembered most.

He had the vague memory of his dad having a kind of shop where he sold seconds—well, more like tenths and twelfths—old clothes, pots, hardware. As he grew up and matured, Fred suspected much of it was stolen. Still, the coppers didn't care about petty stuff like that. So his old man was left alone.

If he thought back to his childhood, he recalled it in sounds and smells; the sounds of the organ grinder, his father's voice as he hawked his wares. The memories were not all pleasant. There were the stinks too, the odors of unwashed bodies—whiffs of vomit and urine in alleys and doorways.

His dad tried to protect him from the ugliness of the place; the angry shouts that signaled a fight that often turned lethal. At one point, he told him he was taking him away. America was to be their destination.

Fred was thrilled when he heard that; he couldn't have been more than ten. He bombarded his dad with questions he couldn't answer. All the man kept saying was it would be good to start over, to begin afresh. Neither one of them could wait to leave.

The day finally came. The ship was called Sea Queen or something similar, he wasn't sure. He didn't recall much of the voyage. He did remember how crowded it was. They were crammed into something called steerage. Again, there were bad smells, vomit mainly. He recalled his father mumbling, 'filthy pigs' more than once.

Going on deck was heaven. His father told him about ships and sailing times. Yes, Dad had been a sailor once, long ago in his youth. He had been to most places but never to America.

Fred recalled sleeping badly and trying to eat, bread mostly—the only thing he could keep down. Two weeks like that, and he ended up hobbling, weak on his feet. Then came the sounds of whistles and men calling to one another, and his father's excited voice urging him on. "We're here, Son!"

And so they were. They saw the Statue of Liberty and Fred cried at the sight. He had never seen anything that grand. But there were things to do. His father warned him. "We ain't outta the woods yet, boy. We have to clear this place and then we're okay!"

There were queues and officials to see, questions and more questions and examinations, too. People were tagged and told where to go. At last, after what seemed like an eternity, they were put into a launch with a lot of people like themselves. That was it. They had made it.

His first impression of New York had been one of amazement. The city teemed with great buildings and masses of people and not all of them poor, either. No, this was something else. The mix was different; sure there toffs, loads of them. And yes, the poor were ignored same as they were back in England—yet his dad said a man stood more of a chance in this big city.

If he had hoped in his ten year old naivety to stay somewhere nice, he was in for a shock. They didn't. No, it was cheap lodgings near the river front. Hell's Kitchen they called it, and Hell's kitchen it was.

Fred sighed. That was enough of the past to remember now. He was tired and needed to think not of the past, but of the future. What lay ahead? Plans had to be made.

If only he were younger. He was no spring chicken at forty-two. Still, he wasn't ready to die yet. And really, he didn't look as old as he felt. He wasn't entirely grey, just a bit at the temples. Of course, he had circles under his eyes and the glow of youth had long since vanished. But there were years yet, weren't there? Sometimes he tried not to think of his own questions and this was one such time.

They had just beat it the hell out of their last stop—that fair in Jonesboro, Arkansas. Why'd the clowns have to kill that nosey kid? He and Happy had a huge flare up over that one, stupid bastard, slitting the boy's throat; he was only twelve. Happy said he'd be trouble and Fred told him off. He called him every name he could think of. He finally told him to take care of the corpse.

"No problem." Happy laughed and handled it like nothing ever happened. The clowns were very efficient. They had enough practice. They knew how to get rid of a body. Of course, it would have to be cut up first. Pig farms were good, as well as swamps—take the corpse's clothes off, burn them, and Bob's your uncle.

The boys, however, were not happy with the moonlight flit; it was one of the few times they were critical of the clowns. Al said they were a real pain in the ass sometimes and Hank agreed. Baby Alice was crying because she had liked the fair.

"Who knows where we'll go, Fred, but I have faith in you," she'd told him. She was all dimpled when she said that and Fred smiled. He even kissed her hand. He liked the smell of her; she always smelled of soap and Johnson's baby powder.

They were soon off, the bus and truck loaded. Pop had to pee constantly so they stopped and lost a hell of a lot of time pee stopping.

This was the second night they had parked here. The checks Fred cashed in town, he'd had for a while. They weren't stolen or anything. They were proper checks, payment for his and his company's expenses.

The boss man was surprised they were going, but Fred used his head. He told him that his ex-wife had served him with papers adding that she was still trying to soak him over a property sale.

"She took it all when we divorced—I don't know what she wants now."

"Yeah," the boss man said. "You can't figure women."

He wished Fred luck and watched them chewing on his stogie as they pulled away. "Our lives are not easy. Take the good with the bad and don't take shit from anyone!" he called out after them.

That was a certainty, Fred thought.

His father cried out in his sleep, and Fred went to sit by the old man. His eyes filled with tears. "You haven't any pleasures left have you, Old Pa?" he said. "I best let you look through your souvenirs. That always perks you up."

It was funny because even though his son was certain the old man didn't remember where any of the souvenirs came from, he still seemed to enjoy looking at the stuff.

# Chapter 3

Fred was up early. Old Pa rose usually at dawn, which was really annoying. Then he'd have a good fart festival and coughing fit, after which he'd give his son a grateful toothless grin. Dressing next, which generally went smoothly. Then, if the weather was nice, Fred would help him outside. It was nice so they went out.

Al and Hank were already there. They had a fire going. "Water's hot," Al said. "You can have your tea."

Fred thanked them and brewed a cup for his dad and himself. Then he sat the old man down and took a seat between him and the boys. "Sleep well?"

They did although Fred could see they looked worried. He knew why. They were all concerned about the same thing; where the hell to go next.

"It's good to cool our heels awhile though…"

Yeah, they all agreed. Well, what else were they going to say?

They didn't speak for some time, not until the clowns began to emerge. They weren't wearing their clown makeup, which always startled the hell out of Fred. Al and Hank were less shocked as a rule. Good thing Baby Alice wasn't up yet because she hated to see them like that, although she'd try not to show it.

It was a funny thing about the clowns but they were always polite—scarier than fuck but polite. Fred greeted them. "Water's hot."

They each mumbled something and took their coffee. Happy commented on the sunny morning and Fred answered him, trying carefully not to look repelled by Happy's skin or his mates'.

It wasn't easy. Of the three, Happy was the most disfigured. His face displayed a roadmap of his horrendous childhood and young adulthood. It told the story of brutality and unimaginable violence.

Happy's real name was Arthur Mundt—not that it mattered. The happy clown face he wore gave him his name. But was he happy? Nah. How could he be? He used to say the best he could do was try not to kill people.

Yes, his life had been too hard.

The clowns met in the Storeyville Orphanage in Georgia. The place was infamous for brutality.

The cigarette burns had long since healed as they had on the others, but the scarring from razors and broken bottles was particularly bad. There was copious scar tissue which had turned deep purple. Jagged lines of it covered his face and ears, too. Poor fucker.

What Fred had pieced together about Happy was, he'd been living with hoboes after running away from home. Cops raided the shithole they were all holed up in and he got dumped at the orphanage as he was under twelve.

Noble and Danny had been turned over to the orphanage shortly after being born. No one told them where they came from. Their names were given to them by a doctor who liked to read. That was why they'd been called Noble Dickens and Danny Shakespeare, respectively.

"We all suffered hell," Happy used to say. "If we weren't used by the orderlies for sex, we were loaned out to their friends. They drank a lot and when they were pissed, they'd really start in."

After a few orphans died, things got better, but not for Happy or his pals. They were good friends by then.

Danny was the most cordial, probably because he was the least scarred. "My face might not show it but all the times I been screwed up the ass—that's what give me my hemorrhoids."

Sad, all of them—Noble had it better. If it hadn't been for the scarring on his jaw and throat, he'd have felt okay about not covering his face up with clown makeup.

"Anyone want eggs?"

The eggs were Fred's surprise. He smiled when they reacted with enthusiasm. "Got them yesterday."

They decided to wait for Baby Alice, but before she came out, the clowns had swallowed their coffee and applied their makeup. They liked her enough not to upset her. They surely didn't feel that way about everyone though.

Fred got the eggs ready. He was already frying them when Alice emerged. "Aw, Fred! You got eggs, ain't that nice!"

"You guys deserve it. I have rolls, too."

It was like heaven for them, what a treat. They had some money now; that is, Fred did and he was feeling generous.

He enjoyed serving them, and when Happy thanked him and really looked as though he meant it, Fred was delighted.

"We have to make plans later. I mean we can stay here a bit longer…but we'll have to hit the road some time."

They knew they would but where would they go? This had been the topic of conversation for a while now. Even in that last place they'd stopped at.

"Any ideas?" Baby Alice asked as she ate. Her table manners were impeccable, considering she loved food so much.

Florida had been mentioned and as they were already in Alabama, it wouldn't be out of the question to head that way. Still, Fred wasn't sure. He wanted everyone's opinion.

There was a lot of shrugging and sighing. No one really knew what to say. Al finally said one place was as good as another.

Everyone agreed. But that still didn't edge them closer to an actual decision. Of course, that really lay with Fred. He glanced over at Old Pa, who seemed a bit out of it today, more than usual. Now he was kind of smiling to himself.

"What's funny, Dad?" Fred asked this in the nicest possible way.

The old man winked. "I been thinking about some old jokes I remember. Serves to make my whole day bright."

When Fred asked if he could tell them any, Old Pa's smiled faded. "No, they just cleared out of me head now, they did. If they come back, I'll tell ya!"

Okay...had to be okay; there was no other way. Just then, Al and Hank started to argue. The boys got along pretty well as a rule. This was unusual. They fought over a woman, which was funny because Hank just wasn't interested in dames. Fred didn't know much else, not that it was his business.

He did think Al and Alice liked one another and that was why she was staring at him now. Since she was, he was denying anything had happened. But Hank shook his head. "You lie! I seen you both—her with her legs spread and you pumping her as hard as shit! I seen your butt cheeks wiggle, you were using such force!"

They both stood to fight. Fred told them to stop it. They agreed. "Look, that's past history, fellas, right?"

It was true. Al agreed so much he was already giving Baby Alice the come on. Fred wasn't surprised when they went for a walk and didn't return for an hour. And when they did, they were both red in the face.

Baby Alice was giggling something fierce but so was Al. Maybe, Fred thought, something could come of it. If only Baby Alice could lose some of that lard, it would be easier for Al when he was in the clinches.

Hank looked over and rolled his eyes a few times at Fred but it was funny more than anything. Even Al chuckled.

"We have to know when we're leaving, right, Boss?" Noble wanted to know and so did Danny. Happy had fallen asleep.

"I'll tell you by dinner time, how's that? Got us some burgers."

"What kinda meat?" Noble teased

"Not human, you pain in the ass," Fred said. "Fucking cannibal."

# Chapter 4

In truth, Fred was worried; he just didn't let on. Folks just didn't have money to spend on anything. It had even begun to occur to him that the whole show might fall apart, that they'd just disband, which was not something he wanted at all.

He was many things. He wasn't particularly honest or trustworthy—in fact he had terrible things on his conscience that bothered him. He'd suffered from nightmares most of his life, nightmares, and the jitters, as he called them. He had no idea they came from things he had done that he no longer recalled.

Despite this, he was affable and fair toward those he worked with. And because they had suffered as much as they had—his show people—he felt downright responsible for them. What would happen to them if they had no home with him? Still, he couldn't afford to keep them as things were. He was down to the last bit of money.

Where would Alice go, poor kid, or any of them? The clowns would wind up being killed one way or the other, and the boys, too. They were out of their heads sometimes. Too fucked up from all they had been through.

As for Al and Hank, they'd eventually broken out of the mental facility they had lived in and joined up with circuses, fairs—whatever they could get into.

Fred ran into them one night when he stopped to pick them up. He had thought they were children. They knew he did and accused him of all sorts of crazy shit. After a while, they came round. It took time though. Both of them had suffered a lot.

*The crew*, as he often thought of them, had been with him for four years. It was two years since the '29 Wall Street crash and things were bad. His father was worse. What else was going to happen? He often wished their luck would change though he doubted it could.

But things did swing another way, as a matter of fact. Yet, there was nothing to indicate a profound change was going to take place. No premonitions of any kind. They were sitting around the fire waiting for their food. Al poked the fire to get it to cook faster. "Yay!" he cried. "It's ready!"

The meat was fatty though because it was cheap but it smelled as good as it tasted. Happy said it was almost as good as flesh, but not quite. The clowns laughed—including Happy.

They were just razing one another. Then they started to talk. Baby Alice spoke about movie stars she liked. She was a real fan of cowboy films.

In the early days, Fred used to sometimes take them to the movies and they'd get the works: popcorn, grape soda, whatever they wanted. No more, though.

Baby Alice asked Fred if he felt alright. He said he did. She looked unconvinced. Fred smiled to show her he wasn't as worried as he actually was.

The food was good and they were grateful for it. After they ate, they stared into the fire as if to read the future.

The boys were shooting crap with the dice they stole from a Woolworths and the clowns were drinking some bootlegged gin. Fred didn't mind as long as they didn't get drunk out of their heads. They weren't good when they ended up like that.

Still, it proved a fine evening, another evening for sitting under the stars and having a decent meal. Fred decided to be positive. Old Pa seemed in a good mood, too when he said goodnight to him and helped him to the truck.

It had to have been past nine when a voice called out. A man's voice. Everyone stopped what they were doing; they just froze and looked at one another.

None of them liked strangers poking round. For one thing, they could be cops. No, they didn't want strangers asking questions. Fred stood and spotted him. A figure was just coming into view.

The man held up his hands. "I mean you no harm," he said. "I just was out walking and I came upon your fire. That is, I smelled it and whatever you cooked…it smelled real good."

Fred didn't know what to make of him at first. Of course, he was relieved he didn't look like a cop. He was dressed kind of shabbily, with a shirt and mismatched jacket, paired with trousers worn at the knees. He was carrying his jacket. "Sure is warm tonight."

Fred agreed.

"Yeah, but that's the way June is hereabouts."

They both reckoned so. Everyone else did also and they continued to as they all sat around the fire chatting. Just then, the man excused himself and said his name was Joe. "Joe Sabba."

Sabba, Fred thought. It sounded like some kind of Hindu name, exotic: Sabba, the Magnificent. Joe cocked his head and said he could read Fred's mind. Fred laughed. "No, really!" he said. "It's what I do. Let me show you."

The clowns started to guffaw and the boys did, too. Baby Alice called them rude and the stranger smiled and thanked her, calling her ma'am, which made her blush. "No, ma'am, I'll show them. You wait. I think you were wondering if I was some kind of magician, Sabba the Magnificent, wasn't it? Is what you were thinking?"

Fred nearly swallowed the unlit stogie he had been gnawing on. "What did you say?"

"I bet I was right!"

Fred nodded dumbly.

No one said anything. It was quite a moment. "Well, sir," the man said. "Looks like I impressed you all. It's just a talent I have. Been like that all my life. Even as a sprout growing up in Amarillo."

Happy was impressed. "Amarillo way? I come from Lubbock!"

"Do tell. Like Lubbock, been there many times." There was a pause although it wasn't a long one. "Carny folk, are you?" Heads began to nod—even Fred's. "I bet you all have a story or two to tell! Nothing like it, fires and storytelling."

That was when it started. A complete stranger broke the proverbial ice. They were soon all chatting for the next three hours, the men interested to learn that Joe had been a carny most of his life.

"Yes, always liked carny folks. Best people there are."

Everyone agreed, including Fred. When Old Pa stuck his head out. "I thought I heard someone different."

Joe Sabba grinned. "Well, hello there, sir. I am mighty glad to meet you. I was wondering when I might."

Fred laughed at that. "Hey, you can't prove you knew he was in there."

Joe agreed. "You are right. Damned if you ain't. But I will say this and let God be my judge—I do surmise that your father there won't go nowhere without his little box of mementos."

Fred winced. He couldn't speak for quite some time. This would be one night during which he wouldn't sleep at all.

# Chapter 5

Fred didn't get spooked often but he sure was now. The most unsettling thing the man had said was the mementos remark. But maybe it was a lucky guess. Even with that thought, which he tried to make a firm belief, he still had trouble sleeping.

What did he know of the stranger? What did he want? He probably just wanted to rest. Everyone deserved a place to lay their head, didn't they?

Fred was pleased with himself when he offered Joe a seat on the bus. The back seat, he had told him, was pretty comfortable, as he could stretch his legs out on that.

The crew didn't mind. They were happy for him to stay, although Fred noticed the clowns looked a bit suspicious of him. Joe just smiled at them. They smiled back, which was something.

If it hadn't been for the mention of his dad's things, everything would have been fine. Maybe it still was. The guy was a character—different. Fred had noticed a look in Joe's eyes though—just a glimpse he caught when he said goodnight to him. It seemed a strange light shone in those orbs, but that proved a fleeting sight nonetheless. The stranger smiled and looked skyward. "Big old moon tonight."

Fred agreed.

"I truly thank you for your hospitality. It is greatly appreciated."

Fred started to walk away, but Joe followed him. "If you need another hand, I am a good worker. I'd do anything …tricks, cleaning, cooking, whatever! I ain't got a roof. Times is hard you know…"

Against his better judgment, he said yes. He left him then and went into the truck. Old Pa had already peed in the pot and Fred emptied it. There was no point in saying good night because his father was snoring by then.

He tried to sleep but then gave up and climbed into the cab to sit staring at the stars. On the one hand, he was worried he'd said yes to the stranger's offer to work for him, but then again—maybe it was an omen to meet up with him. He would add a lot to the show; a mind reader and a magician—couldn't hurt. It would be less of a freak show that way. They might pull crowds in. It was possible. Anything was possible…

Just before dawn, Fred Dodger relaxed and fell into a sound sleep. He slept until Joe woke him up.

\* \* \*

"I hope you don't mind me coming in here… but I did want to speak with you in private."

Could have waited, Fred thought. But he was polite. "No, course not," he said.

Joe handed him a cup of coffee. "Sugar and milk?" Fred nodded. The mind reading again.

The old man was already outside. Joe told him he had seen to him. "He's fine. I gave him some coffee and a roll." He sat down on Old Pa's bed and began: "I think things happen 'cause they're supposed to. Always thought that. I just come from working my way down along the Gulf Coast; didn't get along with the last show's manager. Real bastard," Joe said. "That was in Gulfport."

"Plenty of them around."

"My own fault. I should have stayed where I was. Stupid. Still, we learn from our mistakes. I got a suggestion. You can take it if you like. Times are hard and well, sir, I got some ideas."

Fred agreed. Then he smiled. "I suppose you can tell me what I'm thinking."

Joe waved him off. "It ain't a gift, you know. It's just parlor tricks, hocus pocus, lucky guesses. All part of the bullshit. Where you guys headed?"

"I don't know. Any suggestions?"

"Well, I would say to stay somewhere permanent. I've been thinking about some folks I know, see. They're swell. I'd try there. Your folks of course are included. People will come to see us. You'll see. We'll do alright."

Fred started to feel encouraged. "We'd stay permanent, you mean? No more traveling around?"

"Sure thing. I'd fix us up. Don't you worry about that."

It could work; if Fred had doubts he soon didn't. For the first time in ages, he began to feel really good about the future. It was good Joe came along; just what they needed.

The boys were delighted. "You mean stay somewhere and have shows?"

Baby Alice and the clowns were thrilled. They all said the same thing; they couldn't imagine what it would be like to stay in one place.

Happy elaborated. "See, I've been to places I didn't mind much. But then stuff happened. So many fuckers—people just hate what's different..." He stopped speaking.

Joe reached out and touched Happy on his arm. Happy jumped. Normally, he hated being touched. He didn't move away, which was surprising. He just stared at Joe, who nodded. "Well them days are over, kids. I know. It was meant for me to meet up with you all. I am surely glad I have."

Joe took his seat next to Happy, who poured him some coffee—not something he usually did. It was amazing, Fred was incredulous.

They sat talking, making plans, and when the old man came out, Joe stood up. "This calls for a celebration."

Everyone agreed. Hell, yeah, why not?

Fred felt like a party pooper. "The larder is bare, fellas. 'Fraid not. We'll just have some beer and pretzels if there are any."

"Sounds good to me." Joe smiled. "Let me just go back for my suitcase. My clothes and what not. I left it in a safe place in the woods not far from here. I had my tent pitched. See, I didn't know how far I'd have to go."

Fred took the truck to pick it up, while Joe gave directions. They located the tent and the suitcase.

Fred didn't expect to see the dead man though. Dead as shit with a bullet hole in his forehead.

"Don't mind him," Joe said. "He owed me money. Besides, your clowns and the fat lady will like him, I'm sure."

Fred started to shake, but Joe steadied him. "I knew what they were. I smelled your cooking before, dead giveaway. "Don't look like you swallowed a squirrel whole, boy. I figured them for cannibals. Known so many I find they just give off their own scent. The world is stranger than you know, my friend. And before too long it's gonna get a lot stranger. Meanwhile, let's load my stuff up—including that dead bastard."

\* \* \*

The clowns carved the man up and roasted him. They were very good with their special knives, very adept. Baby Alice was delighted—she made potato fritters. She was able to because Fred stopped for hot dogs and some other things on the way back from town.

"To each his own," Joe said. "I seen a lot of cannibals. They're not the only ones; you'd be surprised how common it is. Most folks just don't know."

# Chapter 6

Fred had often watched Baby Alice and the clowns enjoying human flesh. In the beginning, it bothered him. He even spoke to Alice about it; the clowns were too weird. Alice's eyes had filled up with tears. She promised she'd stop. But because he felt sorry for her, he said she could do as she liked.

She was grateful and he was pleased about that. Damaged people are... *damaged.* Alice's predilection enabled her to get back at the world. Fred was not an educated man but he knew some things.

He knew something about being damaged himself from his own experience. He had suffered greatly in his life. Happiness and contentment seemed always out of reach. Perhaps that was why he cared about his people, despite the monstrous things some of them indulged in.

He glanced up when he felt Joe's eyes on him. As soon as he did, Joe winked at him. Fred thought of him as a winker—his way of communicating friendship, possibly. Still, the man's gaze and the wink were unnerving. "Good grub," Joe said. "The hot dogs. Very tasty." He smiled. "Now, this is a pure guess, you understand. What you really want to know is about the cannibals..."

Fred was too shocked to say anything. The truth was, he did want to know.

Happy and his pals and Baby Alice stopped eating. Clearly, they wanted to hear this.

Joe began: "Scores of people like human flesh! A lot of 'em are carny folk, too. Yup, I met all sorts along the road of life. When I first started I knew this guy—he was supposed to be from somewhere exotic, but he was only from Iowa. The Wildman of Zanzibar, they called him. Loved to eat children."

Baby Alice gasped. "Oh no, no, no. That is awful!"

Joe looked as though he was sizing her up, perhaps to see how far he could push her; where her boundaries were. "Best learn I like to tease." Smiling, he glanced at Happy and noticed him throwing a look at Danny and Noble. They all shrugged. Fred found that worrisome.

"Really, you just don't know what people are capable of. Always said that."

Joe didn't say much after that. No one did, really. Just Old Pa began speaking all sorts of shit, mainly things about London. No one could relate to any of it, except Fred.

Fred explained his father had originally come from the North of England and had gone to London after he was born. The clowns were yawning by then. They usually got sleepy after a big meal though and there was plenty.

Joe stood and nodded to Fred. That was the signal for Fred to follow him where some stuff was hidden. They had to get rid of the bones and other rubbish that hadn't been deemed right for grilling.

With very little talk, they went about their business. They buried it all, as deep as they could dig. "Eight feet ought to do it. We don't want any critters digging this shit up."

Fred nodded. Truthfully, he buried stuff like this all the time—whatever rubbish the clowns or Baby Alice didn't want. Yeah, few things surprised him. He felt himself even getting used to Joe.

They spoke about their plans after Old Pa was tucked in. The crew had been drinking a lot and retired for the night. Fred was pleased because he wanted to discuss things in depth.

Joe did most of the talking. He had been regaling all of them with thrilling tales of fairs and amusement parks he had worked in. The best one, the one he said he'd highly recommend, was Foster's. "That's the one I left recently—and boy, do I have regrets!"

The boys said they thought they heard of it and Fred also recalled the name. "That's almost in the major leagues!" he joked. He was that relaxed.

"That's right! Nearly the A list. Used to be bigger, pre-war, that is. Got started again though in the 20's. Good times for circuses and fairs. Some big acts too, regular circus and sideshow. I used to be the Foster's assistant"

Fred wanted to know why he left. Joe shrugged. "Wanderlust. A fool's desire to move on when he shoulda stayed where he was!"

Fred liked that. "Story of my life that is."

"Well, time to redirect your focus, our focus, the troupe's focus!"

He asked Joe to tell him more.

"Foster's is not as big as it was. Just a few circus acts and hardly a sideshow. No fat lady or anything. Baby Alice is right pretty, too. She'll wow 'em and so will the others."

"You know the owner real well, do you?"

Joe made a waving gesture. "Sure! Didn't just work for him. I was his buddy for years! We used to go panning in New Mexico—you bet I know Tommy Foster. Tommy's a real good buddy. No one better. And he's fun, too; got a good heart. The staff have it good..." He began to speak of the huts then.

"They are great. Not big, you understand, but big enough. And there's a shower block and crapper too just for the show people. There's even a commissary. Your people will love it."

Fred had no doubt. "But my dad—!"

Another wave to reassure. "He'll be fine! Foster's old man lived with him till he died. You and your pa can bunk up, and the others, too—friends with friends like. The only one on her own will be Baby Alice. She's a pretty kid even if she is fat. Where's she from?"

"Georgia way—north part of the state. Her mother died of syphilis the father gave her, apparently. That's when the beatings started. The father beat her cause she was fat so she ran away."

"Ever had a man?" Joe asked with a peculiar glint in his eye.

Fred knew what he was getting at. "She and Al get it on occasionally, I am sure."

Joe flashed a broad smile. "Do tell. Well, if they ever break up—I kind of fancy her, you know. Want to see them jugs. What about you? You ever get any fucking done?"

Although this was a personal question, it struck Fred funny. "Not very often."

Joe stood on his feet. "We'll rectify that! Come on. Let's take your truck. See what we can find. I feel horny just thinking about it all."

\* \* \*

Smithville wasn't far. It was what they used to call a one horse town. Now it had been reduced to a dilapidated crap town with only one thriving industry: the local whore house.

"Guys come from all over. It's got a good reputation, I know! The girls are past it but the madam keeps them clean. She insists."

The house stood near the river. Lit up like a Christmas tree. "They got everything; girls for every sort of inclination, if you know what I mean."

The madam, a big, blousy orange-haired woman did know Joe. She looked delighted to see him. "Where you been, stranger?""

Joe patted her ass. "Back now, baby! Whatcha you got for us?"

"Depends on what you can pay for, my love. No freebies."

"Even for old times' sake?

The madam nodded. "Sorry."

Joe winked, reached into his pocket, and handed her a twenty. "My treat," he told Fred.

That did it. She asked them to both follow her up the stairs. "I got two girls I can recommend. Daisy for you because she likes lollypops and Lucinda for you, handsome, because she likes it any way you want to give it to her."

Fred was in heaven, or at least he thought he was.

# Chapter 7

Lucinda looked about forty but she had big tits and a pretty face. "Let me see what you got, handsome." This she said as she moved in on Fred's fly. He pulled away; she was a little too forward for him. She realized and giggled. "Okay, you do it."

He did. And as soon as his favorite part sprung out, she went to work right away, like a water pump. She got him off in no time. And all the time she was working, he watched her head bob up and down while listening to the cries of ecstasy and joy coming from Daisy's room.

Joe and the whore were having a good time. During a pause, Lucinda asked him what else he wanted.

Since Fred was looking at her tits, Lucinda crept up so they dangled over his face. "Go on," she said. "Enjoy yourself."

So he did. The session lasted for hours. They did it in every position Fred knew and some he didn't that Lucinda showed him.

Afterwards, Joe met him in the hall, laughing. Each agreed he was all used up.

"See, what'd I tell you? Best whore house I ever been in."

They sat a while, discussing their sexual adventures. Joe went first. "The first time I ever been with a woman I was young—not more than fifteen. She was an acrobat in more ways than one."

Joe went on to explain in scrupulous detail just what that meant.

Fred got the giggles after that—and Joe did too, or seemed to. "I like whoring with you, Fred. Not every guy is like you. Some don't enjoy it like you do. Yup. Folks rarely know what they really want. We all have desires. Some folk put themselves up higher than they should. I believe in enjoying everything. How about you?"

Fred agreed despite feeling a bit unsettled about Joe's remark. "As long as we don't hurt anyone…"

Joe appeared to study him after that. But then he smiled. "Of course. Still, there is a lot of enjoyment in what's taboo or supposed to be. I like to study folks to find out what I can about them. Some people have hidden depths they just don't know they had. I like seeing what makes them tick."

"Why's that?"

"It's just a hobby of mine," Joe said. "Just like enjoying a good fuck session with a gal, you know?"

Fred laughed. His judgment might have been a little bit off but that was because he hadn't gotten his rocks off in a long time. All he could think about was how it felt.

"You look mighty pleased with yourself." Joe grinned.

Fred chuckled. "Guess I am…"

Joe slapped his thigh. "Good for you! I have a feeling your fun is just beginning!"

\* \* \*

Fred felt Joe's eyes on him when they drove back. Every time he glanced at him, he found the man watching him and smiling. "There's things you can't even imagine. I saw you were special right away."

"What do you mean?"

"Everyone's different. Some folks have no idea what they're about, what they want, and so on. I can read folk."

"How do you read me?" Fred asked.

"I think you have secrets. Do you?"

Fred nearly swerved. "Hell no, I don't. What do you mean?"

"Now don't get riled up, Fred. I don't mean anything bad. I just mean there are things about yourself; talents you ain't aware you have."

"I don't know what I have. I do know I want what's best for my people and my dad."

Fred fell into thoughts so deep, he never noticed how fast the town disappeared from view. Had he been looking in the rearview mirror, he'd have seen it vanish. In its place stood absolutely nothing.

\* \* \*

When they reached the encampment, they bade one another good night and parted. Al greeted them. "Tucked your dad in earlier. He's sound asleep."

He was, too. Al was okay—Old Pa looked comfortable. Fred didn't think over anything Joe said—he was too tired—but he happened to look outside before he want to sleep. Damned if he wasn't shocked.

Baby Alice was canoodling with Joe. More than canoodling. Joe was feeling her up and she was giggling.

*Shit*, he thought. If Al sees that, all hell will break loose. The boys were little but they were powerful. Fred knew they had killed men for less.

He'd have to set Joe straight. Lay it all out for him. Maybe he hadn't explained it enough—how the boys were. They were little but if rubbed the wrong way, they wouldn't balk at murder.

Suddenly, Joe turned around and looked straight at Fred. Then he lifted one of Baby Alice's massive breasts and began to suck on it. He only did it for a few seconds. Then he turned and winked at Fred.

By the time Fred came outside, Baby Alice had gone. Joe was waiting for him. "She's a peach, skin like silk. Tasty as anything."

Fred was furious. "Look," he said. "Al considers her to be his girl. I thought you understood that." Joe's stare was unnerving. It only served to make him squirm. But still, he repeated himself, elaborated and explained further how hurt Al would be—and didn't Joe understand that?

Joe finally nodded. "I'll stay away."

"Didn't you have enough tonight?"

Joe shrugged. "I am always ready for more. How about you?"

Fred didn't even answer. "Let's just forget about it, okay?" His voice softened then. "Baby Alice has been badly done by. She's been molested countless times. The boss men and yokels—all had a go at one time or another. See? That's why I worry; I want her to be okay."

Joe said he understood. "Well, let's leave it at that. See you in the morning."

Despite Joe's agreement, his attitude bothered Fred. There was something funny about the man—something he couldn't put his finger on. He didn't want to drive him off though.

For the longest time, he hadn't known where to go with his crew. He was seriously thinking about sending them all away and just looking after Old Pa. But he didn't want that to happen. He loved the carny life, so he needed Joe. And really, who was Fred Dodger to have scruples?

If the son of a bitch was randy, let him be randy. Yes, he'd do what he could not to have trouble—but he wouldn't moralize. He slept soundly because of that reasoning. If he was a hypocrite, so be it. Most folk were.

\* \* \*

Fred asked how long a ride it was going to be to Foster's.

Joe thought it would take about two days. "I reckon we need to stop along the way."

That seemed reasonable. "Best eat and go then."

They had a quick breakfast of rolls and coffee and got on the road by eight. There was an air of expectation and it was a happy change. Fred thought Alice looked flushed. It occurred to him that she might be embarrassed about what happened. At least she had no idea their sexual escapade had been observed.

What was it about Joe? He seemed to have a kind of power over ladies. He wasn't young or handsome. He was wizened and he always had stubble. He didn't even look particularly clean and Alice was steadfast about cleanliness. It puzzled Fred, but there was no accounting for some people's attraction.

They had hoped to cover fifty miles and made ninety-eight. The bus didn't go that fast and the truck had seen better days, so it was damned good. They stopped a few times to pee, though. Old Pa always had to go. It seemed they'd just start up and he'd point toward his crotch. Sometimes he didn't make it, waiting that was—the reason why Fred always had fresh clothes ready.

The overnight stop they decided on would be near the Florida state line. Joe said it was pretty. He explained it was just outside Jacksonville and surrounded by woods and a river, and he had stayed there before.

It was great, just perfect. Lots of woodland and privacy. A peaceful place, and the river looked inviting. The boys and the clowns loved it. They even went skinny dipping. Alice looked away when Happy and his mates waved their dicks around. "Stop that. Stop that this minute!" she demanded.

Al warned them too so they finally listened.

Joe did the cook out. They had potatoes and some hot dogs. Some provisions they had stopped off for. Joe's treat. Fred realized he was really trying hard to make up for what he had done. He told Fred he'd been wrong. "I don't often admit it but when I do, you can believe I am sincere."

Fred believed him.

It was a nice evening, sitting out under the stars in the sweet air—talking about Foster's and their new lives.

Joe did some magic tricks. He was really good, too. Amazing stuff he could do with cards. No one could figure out how he did it. Seemed like genuine magic.

He'd ask someone to pick a card, then he'd put it back in the deck, shuffle, and hand the card back.

Happy said, "Yeah, so? I seen this trick plenty of times."

Joe looked at him kind of funny, Fred had the impression he was glad for the question because he looked smug. "Okay, my friend. How about something else?"

He was shuffling the cards when he started to flip them into the air. One by one, they turned over and fell down in front of him. But they didn't fall haphazardly; they fell in an intricate pattern. It was amazing.

"I can make things happen. Remember that."

Fred knew that was directed at him. "Can you? Well, I'll take your word for it."

Joe laughed but looked at him funny. "Okay, but if you ever change your mind… It comes in handy sometimes."

Joe got on more neutral territory after that. He pulled eggs out from behind ears; he wowed them with what looked like a shooting star. It was all fun.

Everyone had a good evening. When Fred saw his father starting to nod, he said goodnight and took old Pa to the truck, leaving the crew sitting outside. How nice to hear them all talk. They sounded happy and relaxed. Fred fell asleep by the time the talking stopped.

Had he stayed up, he'd have seen Hank and Joe go into the woods only to return some time later, holding hands. He'd also have seen Joe bend down to give Hank a long, lingering kiss on the mouth while groping him.

And if he had seen all of that. He'd have remembered Hank telling him how sissy stuff wasn't for him. "I like dames, see. Always have. I ain't no sissy boy."

# Chapter 8

Foster's was everything Fred hoped it would be. A big place—a real circus spread out over four acres.

"That there are the fairgrounds," Joe said. "Let me get Tommy and let him know we're here!"

Joe hopped out to get his friend. Baby Alice and the crew were out of the bus in two shakes, pointing at everything. The clowns got to laughing and playfully pushing one another.

Old Pa even looked as though he liked what he saw. Fred said it would be their new home. And Old Pa smiled more broadly. Joe returned shortly with a man walking beside him. He looked nice, right friendly.

He greeted everyone. Joe beamed. "This is Tommy Foster! I just got finished telling him I made the biggest mistake in leaving him. Tommy waved him off. "Glad you're back now. And glad to see your friends!"

Everyone shook hands and told Tommy how happy they were to be there.

"I could use a good side show. The old one is as flat as a pancake and then some. You guys will do just nicely. Come on! Let me show you around."

He did. They saw the Midway—and Joe was right, it didn't look complete. There was a tattooed man and a sword swallower. That was it.

"Yeah," Tommy said. "We used to have a pretty big sideshow. Just don't anymore. But we'll build it up with your crew. Let me show you the Big Top and some of the acts."

The Big Top proved to be a sizeable red and white stripped tent containing all sorts of circus gear, ropes and pulleys, and men adjusting things—working around the practicing acts.

Tommy pointed. "See that high wire act? That's Ramon and Imelda. They're my acrobats; Spanish, fiery, both of them. Always fighting, damnedest thing!"

He pointed to his new people and the couple waved.

"Nice folks," Fred said.

"Yes, they are. There's a trick rider, you'll meet her later. Her name's Lucy and she's from England! Joe says you and your dad are, as well."

Fred nodded.

"We don't have a big show right now—you know, elephants or anything or big cats. We used to have that sort of stuff years ago. Times are hard now, so I get by with a scaled down show. The acrobats do tightrope and then there's Bob Jarrett and his dogs. They're mighty popular with the kids—trained little poodles and a mutt. They jump through hoops; everyone loves 'em. And what with a better sideshow—it's enough. The tattooed guy is called Lester. The sword swallower is Don. He's a real character. Kind of past it, but he's a hell of a nice guy."

Tommy paused and looked at the crew. "You, ma'am, you're Baby Alice, I understand. I am very pleased to meet you."

Alice looked about to swoon because if that wasn't compliment enough, Tommy kissed her hand. "I worked with large ladies before, but I must say you are extremely pretty."

Al stepped up then. "Alice is my lady," he said. He said it in a friendly way but the words were a declaration of sorts. Joe smiled and Tommy said he understood. "I am glad to hear it. I like when folks are fixed up that way. Find it causes less trouble."

Fred introduced Al and Hank. Then the clowns. Each shook Tommy's hand and said how pleased they were to be there.

"Let me show you the Midway now!"

It looked barren, only having the two performers. Two small platforms held the tattooed man and the sword swallower. They were performing for the few people that stopped to watch.

"It's early," Joe said. "More folks come by later, I bet."

Tommy nodded. "The best time is night time—see them lights?" He pointed toward ropes of lights. "We get them turned on before dusk. It makes the place look magical." Just as he said that, he laughed. "That's something you know a lot about, my old friend."

Joe looked about to blush. He waved him off. "Just some parlor tricks."

That phrase again.

Tommy shook his head. "You're far too humble, Joe. You always were!"

The two lone performers called out warm welcomes to Fred and his crew. They greeted Joe as well. Some people turned around to see who they were talking to.

Joe nodded cordially toward them. He could be quite the gentleman, Fred thought. Tommy rubbed his hands together. "Well, how about seeing the huts now?"

This was what everyone was waiting for, a home at last. Fred didn't know when he'd last had a home—a permanent place to lay his head.

\* \* \*

There had to be about twenty small wooden huts with big wheels, rows of them—one on each side. "See—we attach them to one another when we're moving. 'Course we ain't done that for a year or more. No, I like it here and I think you will, too. The local politicos are pretty good although some are shits to deal with." Tommy paused, looking at Alice. "Sorry, young lady."

She said she understood. He smiled and continued. "Take a look inside."

Alice stepped in first and the others watched from the open door.

"That bed doubles as a sofa. There's a folding table and a cupboard. It ain't the Waldorf, but you'll be comfortable."

Alice raved and clapped. She even sat down gingerly to see if the sofa could hold her weight. It did and she looked relieved. "I love it!" she cried.

Everyone else loved their huts, too. The clowns had bunks and they were pleased with them. Joe said they'd have fresh linen. There was a woman who did chores like that.

Al and Hank were very pleased with their hut. They kept going on about it until Fred laughed at them.

Old Pa cried. He said he didn't want to be alone, but Fred said he'd stay with him and the old man cried again, this time with relief.

"Go get your duds and move in, people. You get three meals a day. Ain't fancy, but it's good grub. Dinner's in an hour."

Fred still couldn't believe their good luck.

\* \* \*

The commissary was located between the huts and the Big Top. The help looked friendly. They waved when Tommy walked in.

"That's Pete. He's been around for years, used to work Coney Island as the lizard man, snake man—or some damned thing. "Didn't you, Pete?"

Pete shouted something but no one could understand him.

Tommy sighed. "Speech impediment. But he's a nice guy and a good worker. All my staff have had it tough. They come here and love it. I try to make it up to them."

"Right nice of you," Joe said.

Tommy chuckled and waved him off.

\* \* \*

The food tasted great. Solid, good stuff—fried chicken and fritters and apple pie.

Old Pa was busily slurping soup with mashed up bread in it. Fred shook his head. "I have never seen my people this happy. You have done us proud, Joe. I am so glad you came along when you did!"

Joe swelled up at that, all prideful and pleased looking. "Shucks, Fred," he said.

"No, I mean it."

Did he ever. Baby Alice and the clowns were laughing—they were so happy—and the boys, too. It was unbelievable how much their luck changed.

When they were finished, they walked around again. Now the Midway was all lit up and there were a lot more people milling about.

"Fair bunch, would you say, gentlemen?" Fred asked.

They didn't agree. "It used to be better but we had more acts like Tommy said. We'll aim for that."

Tommy nodded. "Joe's right as usual. We'll get 'em if we have to drag them here!"

They sat up for hours until Fred nearly nodded off. Tommy was a jolly sort of guy, bristling with enthusiasm. Fred liked him a lot. He liked the sound of his voice and his talk of all the circuses he had knowledge of. "Yes," he said. "It's quite a business. Best there is, in my opinion."

The crew had already gone to their huts. Fred noticed Alice and Al heading for hers. He smiled when they both went inside. Good, he thought. And it was good. It was all good.

## Chapter 9

Fred didn't know when the dream started. He had fallen asleep quickly after seeing to Old Pa. It was the damnedest dream he'd ever had. He dreamed some woman was in bed with him. He felt her mouth and tongue all over him. "What the hell?" he mumbled.

He saw her face then. Just a glimpse in the moonlight. Christ, she was pretty—she smiled and then vanished. When he woke, he felt wetness under him. That was embarrassing; he hadn't experienced that in years.

He stripped the sheet and washed it. He'd hang it outside and if any one asked, he'd say his father peed on it. Shitty thing to do but he felt too stupid about it to do anything else.

Al greeted him warmly. "I had to do that earlier he said, glancing at the sheet. "I was with Alice all night."

"That's great, Al. You both..."

Al stepped closer "I want to give her a ring, to make it official, so she knows. Something pretty but not too expensive. You know, I want to do right by her. She been done wrong all her life."

Fred liked that. "That's good, Al. Really good. I'll ask around where to go. How you fixed for money, kid?"

"I got some saved."

"You two—wow, so glad for you both."

Al gave him a grateful thumb's up and they headed for the commissary. They found the others there. Alice blew a kiss to Al.

36

"Lovebirds," Joe said. Joe turned and winked at Hank, who had his gaze fixed on him. "Don't be jealous. Something will come along for you."

Fred wondered what he meant by that, but Hank just smiled.

* * *

Tommy met them at the Midway, looking exceedingly excited. "Today the guys are going to make platforms. None for the clowns, they'll mingle. I've lined up more performers too. There will be six more small stages. One for Baby Alice and the rest for some new acts. I'm really looking forward to it!"

Joe appeared suddenly. "I remember this place when it was jammed with shows. It's going to be great. Tommy might even get some animals, too."

Tommy just about looked beside himself. "Oh, that would be great. I'd love that!"

"It's needed, I think. We'll start working on it. I got contacts," Joe said.

Tommy shook his head, incredulous. "You're just the best!"

Talented Joe, Fred thought. Always helping. He realized he was becoming almost jealous of the man. What couldn't he do? But it was good he had come along. After all, it was through him that they wound up here.

Later on that day, they met Lucy and Bob, who were practicing in the Big Top. Lucy was real pretty; just Fred's type, blonde and slender. She moved with such grace, he couldn't stop staring.

When she looked at him and saw his attention on her, she looked away. He felt sure she was shy.

He walked over to her when he could. "I understand you come from Lancashire. I come from near there. West Yorkshire, although I grew up in London."

She loved that. They spoke about their homeland for a bit. Then Fred asked if he could watch her practice. She looked at Tommy, who nodded. "Sure," she said.

The clowns liked her. Fred saw them giving her the once over and whispering. Joe noticed and whispered something. Fred figured it to be a warning. What he didn't understand was why they all laughed.

After Lucy finished, Bob and his dogs came in and they were a delight. Everyone liked watching those little poodles jump through hoops, do somersaults, beg, and do it all over again. And the mutt, too—he was a spunky little terrier.

Bob seemed to be a real standup guy. He greeted everyone warmly. Tommy spoke about him. "Bob is the nicest guy. Just has a way with his little doggies."

Bob blushed a little.

"Cutest little doggies this side of anywhere!" Joe joked.

Fred thought he caught a funny look on Bob's face but he wasn't sure.

They had lunch after that and spoke about shows and the carny life. By dinner time, it was decided Tommy would introduce them to his wife. "Mabel will want to meet you all. We have a little trailer not far from your huts."

Fred had noticed a trailer. "I saw it, looks nice."

Joe agreed. 'Wait till you see it inside and wait till you meet Mabel. What a sweetheart!"

\* \* \*

The trailer was tan, trimmed in pink. Outside sat a number of flower pots and little garden gnomes. The clowns were yucking it up, making fun of it. Happy caught Fred's disapproving look and told the others to pipe down, which they did.

Alice and Al were openly holding hands and Hank walked with Joe and Tommy.

Tommy hurried into the trailer. A woman appeared, glamorous and dark haired. She looked way younger than Tommy, probably not more than thirty. Tommy introduced her.

"This is Mabel, my wife. She makes everything perfect."

Said Mabel looked overcome by the compliment and playfully swatted Tommy. Joe kissed her hand. "Mabel, you are the loveliest lady I know."

She giggled and told him he was a charmer.

The clowns looked impressed with her. Fred had already warned them about their behavior so they were polite.

Al and Alice were charming and really tried to make polite chit chat. Alice was never too bad at it but Al wasn't any good. Still, he tried.

There was lemonade and freshly baked cake for everyone. Mabel even insisted on wrapping up a piece of cake for Fred to take back to Old Pa, who had been left sitting outside the hut with the sword swallower. Lester had been kind enough to offer to sit with the old man.

* * *

The clowns, not surprisingly, got to discussing Mabel's jugs but Fred didn't say anything—they had been well behaved in her company at least. So now if they wanted to discuss the size of them, they could. Happy claimed he saw her nipples but Noble said he didn't. "She wouldn't show them like that."

Danny laughed at both of them.

Fred and his people were all sitting outside when Joe came over to tell everyone Tommy had come up with a great idea. If it was alright with Al and Hank, a big man called Dexter, a former wrestler would be part of their act.

"It'll be better for the boys to have something special. Something unique, see? —They can stand on Dexter's outstretched palms... Folks'll love that."

The boys said it was okay with them. Fred was pleased. "It makes it more of an act," he said.

Fred spoke some more to Al before retiring. "I already found out where to go for the ring. Tommy told me about a place near here. The closest town is Dalton. We'll go after breakfast. How's that sound?"

Al was pleased. The two bade each other good night and Fred wondered if he'd have another fucking crazy dream. He kind of hoped he would. As a matter of fact, he started to get hard thinking about it.

# Chapter 10

Lester—tattooed from head to foot and proud of it—told him his dad was fine. "He likes looking at my pictures, as he calls them." He smiled. "Folks do; they always have. That's how I've made my living."

Fred offered him some money for his time, but he wouldn't take it. He said he liked sitting with his father. "He's a nice old fella, just needs company."

Fred helped his dad to bed, piss pot and everything. Actually, he was anxious to go to sleep. He wanted to dream again. He closed his eyes, worried that he wouldn't sleep. But he did, almost immediately.

She was back. He felt her mouth on him, and he came, two or three times. Then he woke up. This time, he pulled the covers off and saw her doing it. Her head was bobbing between his legs and she was sucking him off like that whore had done. When he touched her hair, she went even faster. His heart was pounding and his cheeks felt like they were about to explode. Then, just before he climaxed, she vanished. Poof!

He looked around for her. Sat up and everything. Old Pa was snoring away. Wait a sec, he thought. This is real, this isn't a dream. No, how could it be? He felt it, he saw her. She was there. But it was impossible.

Fred started to worry. Was he cracking up or what? He hadn't had anything to drink. So why the hallucination? He'd have to tell someone. Who could he confide in? Maybe he'd tell Al.

He went back to sleep. *Close your eyes and just relax...* It worked. He fell asleep shortly before dawn and never heard the flapping of wings, which was funny because the demon flew close to his hut.

\* \* \*

The worry hadn't left him when he woke. The dream or whatever the hell it was bothered him. Fred found, throughout his life, if something was weighing on his conscience, he always thought of it upon waking. This he had done.

At least the sheet was dry. He remembered Tommy saying there was a resident doctor on the premises, for falls and illness... those sorts of things. *Well, might as well get some professional advice.*

Maybe he was just tired; he hoped that was the reason.

\* \* \*

Al was wearing his only suit and tie and he looked nice. Fred told him he did, but Al looked concerned about him. "Sleep okay? You look funny."

That did it. He told him in the truck.

"That's some dream," Al said. "Wish I'd dream that."

Maybe Baby Alice had her boundaries, Fred wondered.

Al was staring at him. "I think you're just tired, boss. It's over-work and worries."

Fred said he was going to see the doctor and Al agreed it would be the best thing to do. Al was chatty; in fact he didn't shut up during the eight miles to Dalton. It didn't bother Fred, only amused him. "Everything's going to be fine. Don't you worry one bit!" he said.

"Course I won't," Al said. Except when he lit a cigarette, his hand shook. Fred pretended he didn't notice.

The town was small, just a few shops, not even a movie house. But at least there was a department store. It said Dalton's, the place to shop.

Well, it would say that, Fred thought, because there wasn't much else. He parked up and followed Al, who was so excited, he barely waited for the truck to stop.

They studied the rings in the window. "Look at them!" Al cried. "Damned if they're not the prettiest rings ever. No prices though!"

Fred wasn't surprised he hated when stores did that. Sucker stuff; that was to get the yokels inside and then see how much they were willing to pay.

"Let's go in but I'll do the talking at first."

Al agreed, but he always did. Fred was like an older brother to him.

A ritzy looking saleslady, kind of worse for wear but well groomed, asked if she could help. Fred was glad they were dressed okay.

"We just wanted the price for rings. Don't want anything gaudy. This is for a very special lady."

The woman beamed. "Is it for a special occasion?" she gushed. Fred figured she was thinking engagement rings.

"Yes it is. But we don't want anything too ostentatious…"

"Of course you don't."

Now for the first time, she was studying Al. Fred thought she must have first thought he was a child. When she saw he wasn't, she looked surprised. But she covered it up when she must have felt Fred's eyes on her. A big smile followed. "I'll show you what we have!"

She took out a tray of rings. "These are a very popular line. The workmanship is excellent and the price is quite affordable…"

"What sort of price range, ma'am?" Al asked.

She sniffled. Then she glanced at Fred who put on a kind of don't-shit-us-lady look on his face. "This one is lovely at fifty dollars. That is an eighth of a carat real diamond. You can have it appraised if you like."

Al touched it lightly. "It does sparkle. What do you think, Fred?"

Fred was playing it cooler. But it was pretty.

They did decide to buy it after all. Fred said the young lady it was for had large fingers and the sales lady suggested she come in for a fitting. Al knew Alice would hate that but he agreed.

*Circus of Horrors*

With a twenty-five dollar deposit and a receipt, they made arrangements for Alice to come in the next day. Al was so thrilled but Fred was just hoping that no one would make Alice feel like shit when she came for her ring.

\* \* \*

Tommy was extremely concerned. "Nothing serious I hope…"

Fred said no. Unless, he thought, getting a phantom blow job is serious. Best to have it checked.

"Doc has his office right on site. His trailer is just behind mine. You probably didn't notice it. Best time to see him is around four. He's usually in there catching up on notes. Hope he sorts you out okay. He's very good."

Fred thanked him and left, nearly crashing into Joe. Joe was like that. He just seemed to appear. "How's it hanging?" Joe asked.

That was his favorite expression. It rankled a little. "Fine, as far as I know."

Joe looked mischievous. "Lucinda didn't pull it out too far, did she?"

"It's right where it always is, thank you."

Joe said something back but Fred couldn't hear what it was. There was a lot of hammering going on. Joe told him they were building the platforms. "This place is going to look great! Just Alice's to do—finishing it off, now. What do you think?"

It looked good and the wood smelled nice. Fred was pleased especially because Alice looked overwhelmed. "And I'm going to have a great chair, like a throne."

"You deserve it, babe," Al said.

Joe was smiling and nodding his head. "They're a great couple, aren't' they?" He winked.

This time the wink didn't bother Fred. He was too preoccupied about his appointment with the doctor. Before that, however, Joe was clueing him in on loads of stuff. "It seems to all be happening at once.

We're getting more performers—the show is going to be a lot bigger." Suddenly Joe looked at him. "You alright?

"You're not reading my mind now, are you?" Fred laughed.

"No, course not. Anything wrong?"

Fred explained briefly about having a bad dream and Joe was very sympathetic. "He's nice, old Doc. Good people. None better. You'll see."

\* \* \*

The doctor seemed alright. Kind of squirrely though with thick glasses and wavy hair. He needed a shave and he smelled of cigars and breath mints.

"You must be Fred Dodger," he said, extending his hand. "Tommy's been telling me about you. He thinks very highly of you." He motioned him inside. "What can I do for you?"

Fred explained, leaving no detail out. As he shared the whole thing, he combed Doc's face for any reaction because he feared he was losing his mind.

Doc smiled. "It's merely a dream...but you're worried."

"I am...I think maybe it's my head—like I'm going nuts or something."

"People rarely do that. That's a fear that is more often than not unrealized. Tell me about your life. Are you married?"

For the next ten minutes, Fred told him whatever he could think of. He told him he had come close to marriage a few times but never did go through with it. He spoke of his people, their plans—and their arrival at Foster's. He even told him about the whorehouse.

"And this happened after that visit..."

Fred nodded.

"Seems to me that's it. You were aroused—and your mind envisioned a more perfect creature, someone mysterious and beautiful, like a spirit in the night to satisfy your sexual urges." He smiled. "Why don't you see about socializing? Meet someone nice. There are socials in town...the church..."

Fred chuckled. "Churches and I don't mix."

"Well, perhaps you'll meet someone here. The trick rider isn't married. She's a lovely girl."

The pony girl? She was sweet but she looked so young. Fred asked him her age.

"Lucy's twenty-eight. You're forty-two. Yes, that's younger but she's a nice young lady. Why not talk to her some time? She doesn't have any friends, as far as I know. No steady gentleman."

Fred wasn't really listening. He was too worried. "But the thing… the dream itself. It was a hallucination, wasn't it? That's what's scaring me."

"No. It was just something you willed to happen so strongly, it seemed to have actually happened. I'd just beware of how tired I was if I were you. Take things easier, Fred. And don't worry so much."

Fred thanked Doc Enright and, just as he was about to leave, the man said, "Go see Lucy, it'll be good for you."

Lucy. Hell yeah, she was nice, pretty. And when she spoke, she reminded him of home.

He returned to the Big Top. She was just finishing rehearsals when he waved to her. "Mr. Dodger, hello."

They chatted for a bit, then they went to dinner together. He didn't let any stares bother him. Lucy laughed. "People razz folks around here. Kind of how things are. You know fellow workers and that—like to tease."

Fred knew it was true. He never enjoyed dumplings and stew more than he had sitting there with this pretty girl. They spoke about where they were from and how they came to be in the circus. He didn't want to leave but they finally had to.

They decided to walk along the Midway. It was great walking with her, smelling her perfume. Fred nearly closed his eyes. She was a fine young lady, not a whore. That's what he needed. Doc was right.

It seemed the most natural thing when he reached for her hand. And when he took her to her hut and said good night, he kissed her. But not before he asked her permission.

It was almost a chaste kiss. "I enjoyed that, Lucy. I mean the walk..."
She laughed softly and it was like music.
She watched him walk away and then went into her hut. Joe and Don were already in bed waiting for her.

# Chapter 11

He liked Lucy. He couldn't remember the last time he had felt as he did now. This was no whore. Lucy was a nice kid. Maybe things would work out… Fred didn't want to even think about it because he was fearful. He was a big believer in the jinx. If you want something, then the jinx fucks it up.

How that belief started, he had no idea. Maybe he just felt poor and fearful too long. His entire life had been difficult. Poverty was no stranger to him or to his father. He'd experienced disappointment after disappointment. His father would start a job and then wind up losing it. Fred had no idea why.

"I did the work alright but then they just got rid of me…"

Even as a child of twelve, Fred found that hard to believe. He'd wonder what the matter was. His father was troubled, he knew. This was before he'd told him his most heartfelt secret.

Fred closed his eyes. He didn't want to think of it. That secret and the souvenirs that were central to it haunted him like demons.

Folks have secrets. Joe said that one night. "It ain't nothing to be ashamed of. Just the way things are."

He was always saying things like that. Fred found a lot of what he said helpful but he just didn't know what made Joe tick. If anyone had hidden depths, it was Joe.

Old Pa pointed to his mouth so Fred gave him his breakfast of tea and biscuits. He'd smile at his father and dip the biscuits in the tea for him. Chewing was difficult for his father but he didn't want false teeth—not that they could have afforded them. Would the hard times ever stop?

* * *

It was a fine morning so they went outside. Old Pa looked content if a little sleepy. Fred waved when Al called to him. He liked Al a lot. Actually, he preferred him to Hank. Hank wasn't as open or friendly.

"Morning!" Al called. "Damned if she didn't know something was up. 'Why'd you go off with Fred?' she asked. She wanted to know what it was all about. So I told her. We got to go to town tomorrow. There's something you have to do. Well, Fred. The questions started. She was just driving herself and me crazy. And she didn't shut up. It's just a miracle she agreed to go with us. Cause I wouldn't tell her about the fitting. I want it to be a surprise."

"And she's going?"

"She promised she wouldn't be late." Al glanced at his pocket watch. "She'll be waiting for us if I know Alice."

* * *

She was dressed in a light blue dress with lace and ruffles. Damned if she didn't look pretty in her own way. Fat as hell, like the side of a barn, but pretty.

"Here I am!" she beamed.

Fred could tell even if Al couldn't that she had guessed about the reason she had to go along. That was why she'd done herself up all spiffy.

"You look right pretty, Alice."

"Why thank you, Fred!"

Al agreed. "Blue is your color."

Alice seemed delighted.

Once again Lester sat with Old Pa. Fred had come to count on him. "Are you sure I can't get you something?"

"I wouldn't mind a cigar…"

*One cigar coming up.*

Alice had to ride in Fred's circus bus. She looked a little mortified, dressed as she was, having to sit in the rundown bus.

Fred drove. The ride didn't take long—and everyone was talking, especially Al. At last they arrived. They parked up and went into the store. The same saleslady greeted them. This time she cottoned on. "Show people! I knew it!"

Fred thought it was kind of a tactless thing to say, but he didn't think she meant to be insulting. He said they were with Foster's and she looked delighted. By this time, Alice was dying with excitement.

Al took her aside. "It's for your engagement ring, my sweetheart. I want to marry you some day."

Alice cried like nobody's business. When she got herself under control, she held out her pudgy hand. The ring went on the tip. The sales lady measured and measured and finally said she had it. Then she said it would take ten days for the resizing.

Fred said he'd be by to pick it up. It wasn't until they were outside that they were teased, that is, Alice was called a big fat sow by a red headed kid. The boy looked about sixteen.

Al stared him down and the boy made fun of him. "What's the matter, short stuff, you blind also? How do you fuck that fat bitch?"

Fred told them to ignore it, but it wasn't possible. Alice was crying her heart out. She cried in the bus too and she was still crying when they pulled into Foster's.

"You've just got to ignore people like that," Fred said. "There are rotten bastards put upon this earth to torment decent folk."

Al agreed but Fred doubted he did or could. He spoke to them at length, especially to Alice. "Alice, I want you to know you are a pretty lady and to just have more of you ain't bad at all."

Alice dimpled and despite tears rolling down her face, she giggled. Fred kissed both of her hands.

The only stop they made was at a cigar store. Lester had to have his stogie.

* * *

The newly hired performers started to arrive that afternoon. There were all sorts of folks, including dancing girls, very pretty and young looking, most of them. The clowns got to discussing the size of their tits and who had the best ass. Fred shook his head in a warning gesture. The clowns just laughed.

There was a Gorilla Lady—damned if she wasn't all hairy looking. Fred couldn't believe she was a fake. *Maybe that hair is real.* Dexter, the muscle man, looked like a nice guy, tall and built like a mountain.

Don and Joe stood with Lucy, which annoyed Fred. They looked too chummy for his taste. But any jealousy melted away when Lucy's arm shot up and she waved! She hurried over. "Aren't they all marvelous? Look, here comes the Wildman."

Fred caught sight of The Wildman of Zanzibar. He didn't look very wild or imposing. He certainly didn't look like a cannibal. Fred didn't think he was; probably just more of Joe's bullshit.

"They're all old timers. We worked the circuit before," Lucy explained.

Bob and his dogs were even there. Some kids snuck in and Bob was talking to them. There was a little girl with ribbons he was making a fuss over.

Mabel came out and greeted everyone. She was a fine looking lady and boy did Tommy look proud of her. She knew everyone.

"It's like one family," Fred said, and it was.

He knew then if he had his way he'd stay with them forever. They were nice to Old Pa and seemed to really be one big family.

Tommy had organized a big cook out—kind of a welcome for all the performers. During the event, he made a great speech. There were great eats and the dancing girls came out later wearing scanty costumes. Alice looked at their svelte, shapely bodies. *Poor Alice.*

The girls started to do the hootchy kootchy. Then a shimmy, which got the clowns all riled up. They whistled and clapped. Fred knew he'd have to speak to them about not doing anything stupid.

The others, including the Gorilla Lady, sat with Lester and Don—but Lucy came over to sit with Fred. She was excited about Alice and Al when Fred told her about the ring. Fred wondered if she had ever been engaged. He was afraid to ask her though.

They all had a fair amount to drink, despite Prohibition. Tommy kept quite a store. "And we don't worry about any raids either—I know the right people and money always talks," he said. "Ain't that right, Bob?"

Bob the dog man gave him a funny look. "Sure is, boss."

Fred wanted to ask Lucy about Bob but she was talking to Al and Alice. When Old Pa started to snore, he bid everyone a goodnight. "I best take my dad back now."

They waved him off. But he thought Lucy's wave was special, at least he hoped it was.

He put his old father to bed, whistling as he did. "It feels good to be happy," he said. "Don't it, Old Pa?"

No answer because the old man had fallen asleep. Fred fell into a deep sleep. The distant sound of laughter and talk from the cook out lulled him. It sounded comforting.

But because he was asleep, he never saw Tommy's trailer door open. Nor did he see Mabel step outside, naked as a jaybird. Tommy laughed with glee when two huge wings appeared. "I love when you do that!" he cried.

She laughed too as she blew him a kiss and flew away. Up into the sky she soared, like a giant bird. She came back later—holding a child in her arms.

# Chapter 12

Fred saw to Old Pa. "Come along now, Pop. Let's go to breakfast. It was early; they'd just be cooking it up, but Fred was hungry. Hungry and happy—a good way to be.

They were just having their eggs when Joe came traipsing by. "Did you hear what happened?" Before another word passed out of his mouth, Fred felt his stomach drop. "No, what happened?"

"Damndest thing, Fred. A Dalton kid was sliced up last night. They found him in back of Dalton's Department Store. He was cut so badly, he didn't have an ounce of blood left in his body. Cut his dick off and everything." Joe leaned over. "And whoever did it shoved it in his mouth!"

Fred didn't let his face betray him. "Horrible! Do they know who did it?"

"Not a clue. People like that ask for trouble sometimes though. I've always thought that. How about you?"

Fred replied with some kind of bullshit that sounded right.

"Dalton never had much crime, sure is unusual. I wonder who did it."

Fred shrugged. "Never know what's in people's heads."

"Sure don't."

He sought Al out as soon as he could.

"Did you?"

"Did I do what?" Al asked with a smirk.

"Look, you little fucker. You know what I mean."

Al didn't say anything but he didn't have to. The two stared each other down.

"Look Al, don't fuck this up for us. Don't bring the law down on us, alright? We finally have a good thing here."

Al started to sound off.

Fred understood. "Yes, sure. I hate it too but you can't kill off all the bastards. There are too many of them!"

"Still," Al said. "That's one bastard less."

The clowns were next. Fred was in the mood to sort them out. He found Happy shaving and Noble trying to part his hair straight, not something he generally accomplished. Danny was smoking a cigarette and studying a girlie magazine.

"Is that all you ever think about?" Fred asked.

"Mostly," Danny said. "We don't get to fuck stacked gals very often."

The other two thought that was brilliant and laughed. When they didn't hear Fred join in, they asked what he wanted.

"I'll just come straight out with it. I saw you looking at the new girls..."

"Yeah—so? They're fine looking. I mean there's Alice but she's Al's girl and we don't need so much. Besides," Happy added, "he's never even seen her twat. He takes her doggie style. I seen them once and she don't even..."

Fred didn't let him continue. "Please. It's early."

"Never too early to talk about fucking."

Fred glared at them. "If I hear anything about any one of you doing the wrong thing—or being fresh with those new girls, I will throw you out on your ass. I can get others to replace you."

The penny dropped and they each began to plead.

"No lewd behavior. No fresh or rude horseshit, do you understand me?"

They each said they did as emphatically as possible. It was when Fred left that Happy remarked Fred better get fucked soon or he'd be even more impossible.

The others laughed. "Give me that magazine, Danny. Looks like I'll need it, that and my right hand!"

Noble was thoughtful. "We have a real handicap, fellas. Who'd want to get fucked by a guy wearing clown makeup?"

Happy laughed and confessed that he had loads of girls enjoying his sexual expertise. "And in full makeup!" he said.

Danny stared at him and told him he was a liar. "Oh yeah, I bet I can prove it."

They did make a bet.

\* \* \*

Baby Alice was worried about Al. He hadn't slept with her the previous night. She didn't know what to think. Her head was throbbing and full of memories she didn't want—memories of her father and the beatings, and all for being fat.

She suffered even after she had run away. All the bastards she worked for, all the carny creeps she met along the way, the ones who degraded her verbally and physically; they had all damaged her. But then Al came along and was…so kind to her.

"I'll always love you," she said right out loud in her hut.

And she would. She tried to have positive thoughts then so she began to think of the ring. Fred was going to pick it up for her in ten days! Would they really be married? Al said they would.

It would be all official then. Mrs. Al Harris, she'd be. Maybe they'd get married at the fairgrounds on a day when the place was closed, in summer perhaps. With all her friends there! It would be like a dream! They could probably get a Justice of the Peace to perform the ceremony.

She was just starting to drift off when she began wondering about places to go for the honeymoon.

\* \* \*

*Circus of Horrors*

The clowns were heading over toward the dancing girls' huts. "Look, we'll just talk nicely to them. No vulgarity," Happy said. But even as he said it, he couldn't help but titter.

"Do you think they'll tell us to fuck off?"

They started to get nervous then. Fred's threat was all too vivid.

"It wouldn't be easy to find another show, boys. We all know that." They did.

"Okay, so maybe we should just hope for the best?"

"Hope for the best," Happy said. "You kidding? Let's at least get a whore. Anyone know one?"

Nah, it was hopeless. They turned on their heels to walk back to their hut. "Hey Noble, got enough magazines to go around?" Happy asked.

They were surprised when someone knocked. Happy looked outside. "It's a dame. No, two of 'em, and Joe's with them."

Joe was indeed standing between two of the dancing girls—the blonde and the redhead they had admired earlier. The door banged open and Happy gave each girl the once over twice. Joe introduced them.

"Babs and Freda saw you guys and wanted to meet you."

They were a bit past it. Babs looked at least forty and Freda possibly a bit more. "Hi fellas," they said.

As both women sauntered in, Joe said, "They're clean, don't worry. I paid them for the night—that's if you last that long."

"Last that long? Joe, we've been saving it up a long time!"

"Have fun, kids," Joe called. "Just don't say nothin' to Fred. He's a bit old fashioned although he's enjoyed my contacts."

"No shit," Happy said. "Who wants to go first? I'm ready!"

The blonde giggled and said, "You sure are!" When she started to blow him, he called out to Noble. "You owe me, kiddo. I got my make up on!"

\* \* \*

They got noisy. Joe smiled as he listened to them. If they wanted some willing female company, why not? Poor bastards, scarred up as they were. Hank was standing alongside. Joe smiled at him. "Not for you, huh, kid? This kind of fucking. Tastes vary. What do you think, Hank? Do you think tastes vary?"

Hank shrugged. "Al and I are different, always been like brothers but Al goes one way and I go the other. Life is hard for me anyway." He sniffed.

Joe ruffled the little man's hair. "Cheer up. I got something to show you. I know you've seen some tricks I do but did I ever tell you about my conjuring?"

"Your magic, you mean?"

"Not exactly. Let me show you."

## Chapter 13

Hank was such a good audience. One of the lost. There were many like him; sad, unhappy people. Pissed off at God or something else they might have had store in at one time or another.

Yes, Hank was going to be a fun project, Joe had known that immediately. Some folks were easy pickings, damaged goods filled with enough hate to be useful.

He was still deciding on things though. He wasn't about to rush to judgment, either. The one that interested him perhaps more than any of the others was Fred. Fred, not his senile father, even though that secret of his was fucking interesting. Yes, Joe knew what it was. He knew immediately. But it was the son, Fred, who drew him. He was the interesting one.

Hank was watching him. "Penny for your thoughts."

Joe grinned. "It'd be more than a penny, kiddo." He knew the kid was waiting for a demonstration of his magical skills. "Okay, I know what you want," Joe said as he looked up at the sky. He waved his hands kind of in a hocus pocus way and the moon appeared to get a lot brighter.

"How'd you do that?"

"Magic, kid."

"Want to see more?"

Hank nodded.

This time, Joe raised both arms, shouted something, and a wind began to stir—not much at first but it became stronger until it almost knocked Hank off his feet. "Christ, what is that?" Hank turned around expecting to see damage, but there wasn't any anywhere. "I thought..."

By the time Joe answered, there was no wind at all. "You thought it was real."

"It felt real!"

Joe smiled. "The power of suggestion and possibly some magic, too. Let's see—how about something really spectacular?" Once again, he waved his arms and said something, and animals started to appear. Hank clapped his hands like a child. It was fantastic! Mice and squirrels, small dogs, kittens, but then—! Then suddenly, there were huge animals. Hank's mouth dropped open when the elephant appeared. A big, fucking elephant wearing a pink headdress and everything.

"Queenie! Trick!" Joe ordered

The elephant obeyed that command and stood up on her hind legs. Hank looked on in amazement because it didn't stop there. There was also an elephant handler to keep his charge in line.

And if that was incredible, there was more. Suddenly, cages full of snarling wild cats, including menacing lions and a lion tamer lined up in front of them.

Hank nearly ran from it all, but Joe said the lion tamer had everything under control. "Oh sure, kid. He's as real as the animals. This ain't no magic; this is conjuring—only it ain't trickery, it's real conjuring."

"Real conjuring?"

There was so much noise from the roaring and the shouts of the lion tamer that Hank had trouble hearing Joe's answer. Joe waited until he could be heard. "This is special. Houdini couldn't do this. It was beyond where he was prepared to go, see?"

"But...!"

Joe leaned over. "It's special, like I said. And what's wrong with that? We want a big show! Lots of folks to pay admission. No more worrying about where your next meal is coming from! Now we have ourselves a show!"

Hank started to cry then and Joe comforted him. "Don't cry. You ain't seen nothing yet. You can't imagine the stuff I can do."

"Like what?"

"Like everything. I know what people want before they know themselves. I know for example what you really want. That's cause I know what makes people tick. Who's got love in his heart and who's got hate? I can make people do things, too."

Hank shook his head. "I bet you can't make me do anything."

"Bet I can."

"Bet you can't."

"Okay fella. I bet I can make you do anything I say!" Hank looked doubtful. Joe merely grinned. "You got angry earlier..."

Hank looked about to faint. He had been furious earlier because of a rebuff.

Joe winked and handed Hank a razor. "Go! Do it! You've killed before! He's just gone to pee behind the Big Top! Go on, he deserves it!"

A handsome young man Hank had smiled at had told him if he didn't fuck off, he'd pull his dick off.

Hank stared at Joe, his eyes full of hurt. "Go on and get even, son."

He did. He went where Joe said the guy was taking a pee. The man must have sensed someone watching him and turned around.

"Here you go, you little faggot!" The man waved his dick at Hank. "Too bad you ain't got a camera!"

Hank smiled and pulled out his razor. *Slash, slash*—the man stared at the blood and then at Hank. "You fucking..."

He didn't finish because he started to convulse. When his eyes went open and staring, Hank picked up the penis.

Joe came over and saw the crumpled body. "You done good, kid. Ain't you going to take a souvenir?"

"Hell, yeah," Hank said, holding up the severed penis. "It's a keepsake."

"Sure is. It won't always look like that, son. When it changes you can make something out of it."

* * *

By midnight, everyone was in the Big Top. Mabel and Tommy slapped Joe on the back and laughed with him. Joe had his arm around Hank. "He's my greatest fan," he said.

The couple said they were delighted with everything. "You've outdone yourself, Joe."

Hank felt good with Joe showing him so much attention. He hoped Joe would take him in the woods again and show him his special love.

Meanwhile, there was this circus. He had never seen anything like it—the animals, the dancing girls, and many of the sideshow performers, including Al and Alice, were there.

Alice was moved to tears. "It's a real circus now," she kept saying over and over. "It's like the greatest show on earth! How'd this happen?"

"Who cares?" Hank said. "It's a circus!"

Fred stumbled over. He looked as though he had a few. "When did all this happen? When did the animals get here... and those big cats..."

Clearly he had been drinking because his speech was slurred. Joe was staring at him. Had Fred been a bit more perceptive, he'd have seen the anger in Joe's eyes. "You see this, don't you, Fred?"

"I see it but I don't believe it. It's..."

"This ain't Ringling Brothers... but we've got ourselves a circus. I just wanted to surprise everyone!"

The clowns were yucking it up. "Who cares how they appeared?! We want to be in a show that makes money!"

They all said they felt that way. That universal feeling of wanting to be fed and housed, being part of a great success story was what fueled Joe and all the Joes of the world, not to mention Tommy and Mabel.

Fred was starting to feel a mean drunk coming on. Not something usual for him. For one thing, he didn't drink much and for another, he never had mean drunks; he felt argumentative and nasty.

Joe tried speaking with him but Fred waved him off. "Fuck you," he said.

*Circus of Horrors*

Something passed between Joe and Tommy then, this after Mabel whispered some words to Tommy. It was a meaningful look. Joe nodded and followed Fred out of the tent. He called to him but Fred didn't answer.

The clowns simply watched without saying anything. They liked Fred but didn't want to interfere—didn't want to wind up on Joe or Tommy's shit list. They saw Fred was already on it.

When they got outside, Fred pushed Joe. "Fuck off!" he said and Joe smiled. The smile, to anyone who had seen it, proved a mite unnerving.

Fred started talking to himself when suddenly a woman called to him. He stopped and came face to face with Lucy. "What do you want?"

She took his hand but he shook her off. He nearly said fuck off but he stopped himself. Despite the state he was in, he didn't want to be rude to a woman.

Besides, she looked so pretty standing there. He could just make out her face in the moonlight. "Fred…"

Her voice sounded funny in a crazy way, enticing and haunting all at once. "Fred…"

And why was she wearing that white dress? Didn't she know her tits and bush showed with that thin material she was wearing? She was usually so demure. He kept staring…couldn't help it.

She started to speak, telling him nice things. He heard her words, just a few about how she liked him and didn't want him to be upset. And he was pleased but he didn't care about what she said.

She took his hand finally. "Let's go to my hut," she said.

He let himself be led away by her. Each step they took, he imagined what it would be like, how her skin would feel and taste.

When they got to the hut door, he kissed her. He didn't remember kissing a woman like that in years—not since his youth. She responded, too. She told him things she'd do for him. He watched her open the door.

"Fuck me, Fred. Do whatever you want to me and I'll do it to you…"

\* \* \*

Joe stood back by the tent with Tommy and Mabel. "I bet we don't see him until noon, tomorrow," Joe said.

"If then," Tommy added.

"Want to come in for a night cap?" Mabel smiled.

"Sure. Only we have to clean up something. Mabel, you still do those casseroles with mushrooms and fennel? I've got the perfect meat to go with it."

# Chapter 14

Joe shook his head when he heard Hank calling for him. "I better see what he wants."

Hank looked desperate. Joe tried to sound pleasant but his voice was edged with anger. "Me and the bosses got business, kid. We're going to take care of that mess you made earlier, don't worry."

Hank felt his heart drop. He didn't want to be reminded of what he had done. Besides, hadn't he done it at Joe's urging? No, perhaps not.

"But I need you, Joe."

Joe grinned and put his arm around him. "I am your friend. We're pals, aren't we? Well, perhaps more than that." He winked. "You and your buddies—all of them, Fred too, will be okay. The lean times are over."

If someone without Hank's horrific childhood or experiences sought to question any of this, Hank did not.

Joe smiled. "You know, you're special to me. You always will be. I'll see you very soon, my friend. Be happy. It ain't against the law, right?"

\* \* \*

It was all bullshit. Al was spouting mad, addressing everyone. The whole fucking circus was standing there, even the newly arrived lion tamer. Al had already thrown a thousand questions at him.

*How'd he just show up?*

*Where was he from?*
*Where'd he work before?*
Clarence Middleton answered every question and, considering the circumstances, was in good humor, only interjecting a few times as to what all this was about. "It feels like an inquisition," he said.

Al had no idea what the fuck that meant and he didn't care. He just went over old ground. "Hocus pocus and the words of an old carny cannot make things appear! We joined up and there was a pony and some dogs. Now we have one goddamned elephant and wildcats, for Christ sakes. And we have you! Where'd it all come from?"

Clarence once again said he was from Detroit.

Al just looked at him. Baby Alice was trying to calm her fella down but wasn't getting anywhere. The clowns didn't give a shit. Happy said so. "I just don't care—who cares, really?"

That got a lot of nods and answers of the affirmative persuasion from everyone with the exception of Al and Alice. Alice, ever the loyal fiancée who had yet to get her ring to fit her finger, was pleading with Al to calm down and for everyone to not shout at one another.

But Al wasn't through. "And you," he said, pointing toward the elephant's handler, "who the fuck are you?"

The handler was young, didn't look more than eighteen. He smiled. "My name is Anadi. I come from India."

Al waved him off and shook his head. "I just don't get it."

Hank, feeling unusually positive because of what Joe said, agreed and took it upon himself to try and make amends with his former best friend. He used the same tactics that Joe used on him but it didn't work with Al.

"You're all nuts!" Al said. And he stormed off.

Alice set out after him. She would have run if she could have—but she couldn't. Walking was difficult enough. But she tried to go even faster. She called to him but he didn't stop. It wasn't until she fell over that he did. It wasn't because he had eyes in back of his head and he saw her fall over; he didn't. It was what Hank screamed—"Alice is dead!"

*Circus of Horrors*

Hank was kneeling down and holding her hand. He had already surmised there was no pulse. Several others including Happy and a few of the dancing girls were in agreement. There didn't seem to be a pulse.

They made way for Al as he rushed over. He cried and called Alice's name. When he didn't feel a pulse, he put his head on her chest to see if he could hear a heartbeat. Nothing. Someone got Doc.

Doc tried a lot of stuff and nothing worked—but then Joe appeared. "I'm something of a healer," he said.

Al was no longer cantankerous. He looked open to just about any help.

Doc said he thought it too late, but Joe persisted. He put his hand on Alice's head and prayed. And he prayed a long time, too. He prayed despite Al shouting Alice's name and screaming his head off.

It was when Joe said a particular thing that Alice sat up. She looked to be dopey, but that was all. She was alert and, most importantly, she was alive!

Al saw and nearly fainted. If it hadn't been for Happy catching him in his arms, he would have. Happy asked him if he was alright because he started to convulse. His entire body was contracting and his eyes rolled back. "What's wrong with him?"

Soon, a whole crowd surrounded them including Alice, who was just fine by this time.

Joe stopped it by just staring at him, it seemed. When asked about it, he said he didn't do anything. "Just a kind of prayer of mine."

As for Al, he regarded Joe differently now. The man was like an angel or something.

\* \* \*

Fred finally staggered out of Lucy's hut just before dawn. What a time that had been. He hadn't worked that member of his out like that in years, not with anyone nice. She was the girl for him, alright. He hoped it might come to something permanent between them. And if not, an occasional session with her would be better than nothing.

He was smiling to himself when he noticed all the excitement. There was a crowd. Something had happened. He wanted to know what was going on. Hank started talking a mile a minute, explaining things, but Fred stopped him.

Doc Enright and Happy appeared then. "Please, Fred. The young man's right." Doc went on to explain about Alice and how he couldn't do anything, adding, "But then Joe came over and did his healing."

Fred put up his hand. "Now he heals—what the fuck is he? How does anyone accept this crap? I sure as hell don't."

Happy tried to explain. "The elephants, I agree—it's nuts, but who cares? It's a living…we were fucked up! No home—just the goddamned bus. No prospects. How much longer could we exist like that…?"

Happy stopped speaking mid-stream. He wasn't exactly fearful of anyone; it was the expression in Fred's eyes that did it.

Fred spat and told him to leave him alone. "I've had enough of this crap. I've seen carnies before—I know what they can do." His voice was flat when he next spoke. "This is different. This feels wrong…this is fucked up!"

He walked off after that with Happy and Doc watching him.

It wasn't until he got to his hut that he saw Old Pa standing outside, doing something. He couldn't see very well so he ran up. "You alright…?"

The words just stopped. That is, his voice cracked and despite his lips moving, nothing came out, because there in front of him was his father holding up one of his prized souvenirs.

"No!" The strong box! He had secured and locked it, put it under the floor of his pickup. No one knew about it, not even Old Pa with his brains being scrambled as they were. Goddamn it!

"Old Pa, how'd you get that—?"

He was just helping his father to stand—not mindful of all the babbling shit the man was spewing…when he saw Joe watching him.

It was then that Fred felt his heart stop, *really* stop. It only happened for a couple of seconds—but it did stop, of that he was certain.

# Chapter 15

He couldn't move right away, so he just stood there like he was paralyzed. The strong box was open and the souvenirs spread out; dropped when Old Pa was distracted. And there was his father holding up each and every one of those damned things.

"Stop that!" he ordered. Old Pa, looking fearful, dropped what he was holding and began to cry.

Fred couldn't believe it when Joe sidled over. "Anything I can do to help?"

Before Fred could say anything, Old Pa headed for the souvenirs again, but Joe beat him to it. "What's this?" he asked, picking something up. "Can't tell in this dark. Your father's?"

Before he could do anything, Old Pa grabbed the piece of fabric from Joe's hands. "Mine."

The old man very rarely asserted himself. This was unusual. Joe laughed. "It's alright. I'm not going to touch it again."

Old Pa turned his back on him just as Fred found his voice. "He's had those things for a long time." His voice sounded flat and weak. "They're just things he collects. Worthless rubbish, but important to him, I don't know why."

"No kidding. Well, it's good to have keepsakes, I reckon. Although I will say, he seems to take quite a store in them. Wonder why that is. Would you venture a guess?"

Fred barely answered him. He knew he was being baited. "I have no idea. My father is senile, as well you know. He takes a keen interest in things others would call worthless."

"You sure about that?" Joe asked.

"Of course, why wouldn't I be?"

Joe asked if he could touch one. "I had an act once…"

"Yeah! I can guess. Your mind reading crap bullshit act, right?"

"You're hostile, Fred. Why so hostile?"

Suddenly, Fred felt a pain in his chest.

"You alright, Fred? Why are you holding your chest?"

"I'm just fine. I'll be taking my father in now."

Joe called out goodnight and began to walk away. He stopped though and turned. Then he waved and was gone. Fred watched him until he vanished from sight. When he did, he put his father to bed.

\* \* \*

There was only one thing to do. He'd put that fucking thing away where no one would find it. That stuff? Christ, he had no choice. And if his father asked about it ever, he'd say what he always said—that it was in a safe place. The thing was, it had been in a safe place; only, Joe had found it.

Fred hated shit like that. Nosey old git. What was he poking around for?

Actually, his feelings about Joe went beyond mistrust. Now he feared him. That carny shit—magic—what the hell was that? It had to be some kind of trickery, but still—! Joe gave him the creeps. He just did. Of course there were reasons for that and they concerned his own secrets—secrets he didn't want divulged. Secrets he had on his conscience.

But first things first. The main thing that concerned him now was the contents of the strong box. And there were very good reasons for that. They didn't bear thinking about, though, so he dismissed the thought from his mind.

"Old Pa," he said. "I have to go out for a while but I'll be back."

His father blinked at him with those vacant watery blue eyes of his. He had probably already forgotten about the souvenirs.

"Right," Fred said as he slipped outside. He'd roll out of Foster's quietly with the motor off. Once he was on the road, he'd look for the right place to bury that fucking box full of his father's sins.

* * *

He tried to think rationally. To be cool-headed was the only way. He had a shovel in the pickup he would put to good use.

He drove for about twenty minutes. It was just starting to get light when he turned onto an old road that looked as though it was never used. A tree lay across it, probably felled in a storm. It took him a while but he moved it.

He got out and walked around. There was nothing as far as he could see, no house or building of any kind. He felt certain this was the perfect place to bury the damned box. He looked for a landmark. Not easy, there being only trees and bramble. But then he spotted some huge rocks, more like boulders. Perfect.

He buried it there, right in front of the largest of them. He left but not before pulling bramble and all sorts of grassy crap all over the freshly dug earth. As safe as houses, he said to himself.

* * *

Old Pa was awakened by the sound of a woman's voice. When he looked, he didn't see anyone at first, but then his sight adjusted. He asked who she was—smiling as he did because as dippy as he was, he liked company.

She didn't answer though, just came closer. The thing was, she *floated* toward him, her feet just inches from the hut's floor. He didn't notice though.

He did see that she seemed to be reaching out for him. Someone else most likely would have been scared shitless but not Old Pa.

He started to speak—just nonsense. He couldn't form whole sentences any more as his brain wasn't functioning, hadn't been for a long time.

She kept coming closer, but stopped moving when Fred got out of his truck. And when Fred turned the door knob, she vanished as quickly as she had come.

As soon as Fred came in, he knew. The ghosts were going to start coming again and all because of the souvenirs!

# Chapter 16

Al had gotten Doc Enright when he heard the screaming. It happened during the night. "It's coming from Fred's hut!" he said. "I knocked and knocked but he wouldn't open the door. I'm worried."

Enright asked Al to wait outside while he went in. He came out some minutes later. "I gave him a shot, something to calm him down. I'll have someone come to sit with him. He didn't sound too coherent to me."

Enright asked Al if he knew of anything that had happened to cause his friend to act like that. Al said no.

"Well, I wouldn't worry. He'll probably be fine. Looks like nervous exhaustion. I'll look in on him later."

Al liked the Doc. He knew he was friends with Joe and that was good enough for him. He told Joe about Fred's trouble. Joe looked upset. "Poor guy. Too much stress and worry; it'll get you every time."

When Al told him Fred was supposed to drive Alice and him to get the ring in town, Joe said, "No problem! I'll take you both."

Joe spoke his head off during the drive over there. "You kids, I'm so happy for you. Nothing like love. I never had the good fortune to find the right woman, although I have had fun in my time."

Alice giggled and Al smiled. If his life had been full of darkness and pain, Joe had come along to push all that bad shit away. Al never forgot hurt or kindness and besides, Joe had saved his girl. It was like a miracle or something. "It's nice of you to drive us, Joe."

"I love you guys. We're friends, right?" Joe watched them in the mirror. "Friends like us have to stick together."

Al agreed. "Sure do…"

"It's a tough world for carnies like us."

Al's eyes filled with tears. Joe's approval meant a lot to him.

Alice reached for Al's hand and squeezed it. "Should I tell him?" she whispered.

"Tell me what, girl?"

"Well, I had this funny dream last night. Never dreamt anything like it ever." It was obvious she found it difficult to continue.

Al hugged her. "Go on, honey."

She came right out with it then, just a tumble of words. It was easier that way. "I dreamt I was beautiful! Honest! I really was. I kept looking at myself in the dream, you know, and I wasn't me—I was like one of them Hollywood actresses!"

"What's wrong with that? That's a nice dream! You hold on to that, sweetheart! Dreams are good. They can come true!"

"If only…" Alice sighed.

She didn't notice Joe staring at her in the mirror.

\* \* \*

The ring fit! Al was getting his wallet out when Joe said, "No, kids. This is on me. And no arguing!"

Neither one of them could argue; they were speechless. Kindness was a rare thing to them. Alice couldn't stop crying and all Al could do was just watch Joe pay for his girl's ring. He did manage to say he had never known anyone as generous or kind. "And that includes Fred," he added.

Joe liked that. It meant a lot to him. In fact, it meant everything to him.

\* \* \*

They had a little celebratory party in the commissary for the happy couple. Even Mabel and Tommy attended. Mabel said she was going to see to it that they were married on the grounds, if they liked.

That was when Hank nearly lost his balance. Hank was well drunk. He had more than a few while they were gone. Homemade shit—the clowns were astute makers of moonshine. Hank had that and some cider that the Gorilla Lady made.

It was when Hank began talking all kinds of shit that Al got worried. They weren't exactly choir boys. They had killed a number of people, probably at least as much as the clowns had. Although they hadn't eaten any of them. That made them a bit more human, Al reasoned, than the fucking clowns.

Hank started the litany with regard to the body count they were responsible for, but with his slurred speech, it was all pretty indecipherable. When he was assured everyone was looking his way, he continued to ramble.

"Remember old buddy that bitch nurse at the mental hospital? I cut her throat and you sliced her head off. I wanted to, but you did it… That's why we high-tailed it outta there!"

Tommy and Joe were shaking their heads, trying to reason with Hank. "Now, now, Hank," Joe said. "Let's get you to bed."

That was when Hank started to cry. "Bed! But I want you to be there, to stay with me! I need you. Oh, how I need you!"

He broke down then and everyone knew what he meant, including Joe.

"We're good friends, kid, ain't we? Sure we are. Joe tried to placate him but Hank was too far into a crying jag. He just couldn't get a hold of himself.

Al offered to help his old pal go back to his hut but at that point, Hank got violent. "Look, you little bastard. You're leaving me for her, for that fat bitch! You've never loved me. You said you did, but you don't!"

Al exploded. "Don't say one word about my Alice! I love her! We're going to be married. I'm not like you, I love women—you never did!"

Hank ran off then. Joe shook his head. "He'll calm down," he said. "I'll see that he does."

\* \* \*

Alice had been very hurt by what Hank said and it took a long time for Al to calm her down. At last, she did.

Joe took her hand. "Honey, you are blessed," he said. "And despite Hank feeling the way he does, he is as well. The hard times are over, kids. We're going to make a success of this circus. I got big plans. In fact, there is going to be a big meeting tomorrow night. Tommy and Mabel want everyone to attend."

Joe stood smiling at the happy couple. When Tommy looked at him, he winked. Tommy winked back.

\* \* \*

Fred slept most of the day. Old Pa was alright. Lester came to sit with him. Later, he said he was going to the meeting. He asked Fred if he wanted to go, but he said he'd rather get root canal than do that, eliciting a laugh from Lester.

Before the tattooed man left, he brought Fred some stuff from the commissary. Fred picked at it. His appetite hadn't returned but he was feeling better. He had just come back from taking a pee when he happened to see Joe slip into Hank's hut. The two were as thick as thieves, he thought, and probably much more than that.

# Chapter 17

Hank didn't care about his head throbbing. Nor did he even mind Joe had already left. It was okay because something great had happened; something unfathomable.

Once he had seen a movie—about Christ. It had made him cry, it moved him so much. In time, he'd forgotten about it as all the darkness in his life ensured he would. Now, though—this particular morning—Hank saw the light once again. He also heard the music, not real music, just a feeling of exhilaration in his chest.

An educated person might have referred to it all as an epiphany. For this Friday morning in Hank Brown's shitty circus hut, he had undergone something like St. Paul's conversion on the road to Damascus, with one difference. He didn't hear God's voice; it was Joe's voice he heard.

*Hank, my boy, I give you love...!*

*Yes. Oh yes! You do, Joe—and it makes me whole, a complete and satisfied being. I will do your bidding, whatever you say—I will be your instrument... serving you always!*

He dressed and shaved. And for the first time in his miserable life, he did not hate the face that stared back at him. He didn't see the bulbous nose, caused by his father's beatings—nor did he see the gaunt, singularly unhandsome face. He did not hate his coarse hair that broke many a comb. In short, he was so pleased with himself, he actually smiled at his reflection.

Even when he finished dressing, he did not stare with repulsion at his small feet encased in the boy's oxfords he wore; there was no shame in him, no feelings of hurt or anger or apology.

Hank had never felt good about himself in his life. Now he *did*—it was great but a feeling he'd have to grow into. Someone once told him people who suffer have to get used to the good sometimes. Now, he knew that was right.

He clutched his chest as his eyes filled with tears. "I am happy now… and I always will be!"

He found Joe in the commissary. When Joe smiled, Hank thought he saw a light around his head, like a halo. It only lasted for a moment.

When Joe offered to get him breakfast, Hank said he had never been hungrier. They ate together, just the two of them, and when Joe spoke about the big meeting, Hank listened with rapture.

Happy and the two other clowns joined them. At first, Happy teased Hank, but when he caught a look on Joe's face, he stopped.

Joe bade the others as they came in to join him. Soon, it looked like the depictions of the Last Supper with Joe in Jesus' place.

There were questions, but Joe put them off. "It will all be discussed later in the Big Top, don't you worry about that."

\* \* \*

The Big Top! Now it really deserved to be called that. Tommy's men had already set up Ramon and Imelda's high wire and trapeze. They were just finishing up their trapeze act when Joe waved to them. Imelda waved back just before she swung away from one trapeze to another.

It was all quite thrilling and the other performers, Bob and Lucy, applauded.

Everyone took a seat wherever they could find one. They shouted hello when Tommy and Mabel came in.

The sideshow performers were there, including Al, Alice and Hank. Mabel told Hank how spiffy he looked and Joe agreed. "He does, don't he?"

When she wanted to know where Fred was, Joe said that he had already seen to his father. "I have one of the men watching him. You know to make sure he's alright. I bring him his meals."

"And Fred, how is he doing?" Mabel asked.

"Doc thought he might need some more rest."

Just then, a look passed between Joe and Mabel, but no one caught it.

\* \* \*

The meeting soon got underway with Tommy never looking happier. He and Mabel hugged before he started. "I can tell you folks, it's all happening! We should be ready to open Saturday! Two shows—afternoon and evening. The Midway is already done. Our men," he nodded to the batch of workers he relied on, "are just the best bunch of fellas in the world. I've known them for ages! They have been with me from the beginning."

The guys waved and whistled and looked delighted when most of those assembled applauded.

"We'll be having some guests for our opening, dignitaries if you please." He paused and looked around for effect. "His honor the mayor will be here with his good lady wife and some assemblymen. Mabel and I are very excited! The rest of the week is important, loads of rehearsing and preparation. I know you all know what hard work it takes for a circus to function, and because you are such seasoned performers, you are invaluable to me!" He gestured for the dancing girls to come up.

"Now, I want to introduce each of our four lovely ladies by name. Just in case you don't know. This is Maggie, she's the baby—after her there's Babs and Freda!"

All three were very attractive brunette, blonde and redhead. The fourth, a black haired beauty, was the most attractive. "This is Dorinda, their lead dancer. Tell the folks about your dancing."

Dorinda looked about to die but she did. She rattled off show names and fairs and even mentioned being one of the dancers in Showboat, when it was on Broadway. That brought the house down.

There was more to announce after that. Lucy and her ponies, and Bob and his dogs, as well as Imelda and Ramon were all given times for their acts. Tommy paused. "Now, Clarence, our lion tamer, and Anadi, Queenie the elephant's trainer, you guys are great!"

Clarence waved and Anadi beamed.

"Then there's you fellas…"

He meant the clowns. "The acts go one after the other with you guys milling around being friendly and funny with the audience."

The clowns liked that. Noble was being facetious when he pointed out they were good at milling."

Tommy just laughed and waved them off. The rest of his talk focused on the Midway and being on time and being courteous. "And," he added, "We have our own security folk to deal with people that are rude or threatening. Yes, sir! That's one thing Foster's will not take. We never have and we never will!"

More applause and cheers at that. Even Joe put his hands together and clapped like anything.

If there was one thing that seemed out of synch, it had to do with Bob.

Hank wondered why Bob looked so unhappy. He asked Joe about it.

"It'll be okay. I have to sort something out," Joe said. "Sometimes people don't know when they're well off. I just think Bob isn't happy here anymore."

Hank said he didn't understand that.

Joe smiled. "I'll see what it is and make it right!"

If Hank worshipped Joe before, he worshipped him even more when he said that.

# Chapter 18

Were the ghosts back? Fred didn't dare tell Doc Enright. He just said his nerves were playing up. Doc understood that. Fred was certain the doctor wouldn't understand about the ghosts though. Especially when they were spirits of murder victims; women killed by his father! What they would do to Old Pa didn't bear thinking about.

Knowing they most probably were back and not being able to do anything about it was torture. But it was his life. It had always been like that.

He went over a lot of old ground. *Were* there ghosts? Could there be such a thing as ghosts? He didn't really think so. But he had questioned it many times in the past. Things moved sometimes on their own. At one time, he thought he'd go crazy. Maybe he was or if he weren't he would be.

And now it was worse. A lot of strange shit was happening, like that crazy dream he had about the dame in his bed. Could that be part of it?

He brewed some tea for his father and himself. They even shared biscuits with jam. Fred wasn't ready for the commissary yet.

He knew he had to confide in someone and Al was his friend. Al trusted him enough to tell him his own story. And because he did, Fred had come close to confiding in him many times over the years, but he hadn't done it—hadn't because what? He didn't really trust Al? If not, why?

*Circus of Horrors*

*Christ sakes, Al!* The little guy had poured his heart out to him many times. How many nights had he comforted him? All through the many years he had known him.

Fred shook his head. He didn't want to give way to tears because if he started now, he'd never stop. Yeah, there were a lot of sad and poignant memories. Memory Lane was packed with them.

Old Pa wanted to get dressed so Fred helped him. "After you're dressed, what say you we sit outside?"

The old man gave no reaction. Fred felt certain he didn't know him now. "It's okay, Pop. It'll all be okay."

They were sitting outside not ten minutes when Al appeared. "Missed you at the meeting, Fred. How you been?"

Fred shrugged. "Okay…"

"It sounds pretty good—all of it, you know. According to Tommy Foster, that is. Show's supposed to start Saturday…" Al stopped speaking and studied Fred. "Are you alright? You don't look so good…"

Fred smiled sadly. "I just need to tell you some stuff." He glanced over at Old Pa who had suddenly started to sing some old English music hall song.

"I remember you when I was a boy, Pa—and you were okay. Before your stroke. Remember the voyage?"

The old man didn't recall anything. His eyes looked blank. Fred bent over and kissed his father's head. "I'm just going to speak to my friend a moment. Be right back."

They had only walked about a hundred yards when he told him. "My dad killed some people, Al—a long time ago."

Al looked incredulous. "You know my history… Your secret is safe with me, my friend."

Fred nodded. "But there's something else. It's happened in the past but not for a long time…"

"What's happened? Tell me…"

Fred just came right out with it. "Do you believe in ghosts?"

The thing was, Al did, but not in the way Fred meant. "We all have our demons," he said. "But ghosts no—not really. I mean, if I did I'd be expecting a thrashing every night from my dad. Oh yeah—he died. I heard he did. Someone told me, a neighbor I think it was. He said, 'Your old man is dead now. His rottenness had its way with him.' "

Fred wanted in the worst way possible to ask if at any time Al had been frightened of a noise or something he couldn't explain. "You know, did you ever get spooked..."

"Thinking it was my father, you mean? Nah, not really." Al was studying him once again. "Don't be frightened, Fred. There are things we can't explain... Did something happen, though? You might feel better if you told me."

Fred couldn't reply at first. But then he finally did. "See, Old Pa kept some things...souvenirs...and I think..."

"That it ties in?" This was something Al was familiar with. The two had often discussed their past employment. "I told you about the clairvoyants I knew but it was fake carny shit."

"But Joe—!"

"Joe? What do you mean?"

Fred told him about the strong box.

"And so you buried it."

"Yeah, but as I said—the damned thing was hidden in the pickup. It'd been there for years, Al. No one found it. Just Joe."

Al shook his head. "Joe's just a trickster. Yeah, he found it after searching the truck. See, that's how them guys work. They find something out without the person knowing—or realizing they are getting information they need. They do it all the time. Shit! There was a guy in Des Moines who used plants in the audience—when he'd fleece suckers for the long lost relatives, asking things that it appeared he knew. He made a lot of money. I think that's a shit con, though."

Fred still looked worried. "But there was this chill in the hut, when I got back from burying the box—a chill that I'd felt before. That last time it happened I had seen something. Stuff moved and I heard a whisper. I didn't sleep for days after it."

"But you got rid of the box now. It's tied in with it, right? I mean I don't really think this can happen, these ghost things, but as long as you no longer have it around, it should ease your mind that it can't happen. The tie is broken, see?"

Fred was so relieved, he cried. "I never thought of it like that. It's so simple!"

"Ain't often things are," Al said. "But now that there's no box... there's no ghosts. He's okay, Joe is. Look how he helped my girl."

# Chapter 19

Al was right. It was like Fred originally had Joe pegged. He was a phony of the tallest order; a trickster carny man, nothing more, nothing less.

Fred didn't know how old he was but he figured Joe had been around for years, enough time to pick up a lot of carny con stuff.

Sure, he reasoned. The man was a fraud—nothing to him. Like cotton candy—all blown up but melts away to nothing.

He hated him, sure. That sob had snooped around until he found something hidden. It was obvious. If you look hard enough, you find stuff as he had done with the fucking strong box.

Ghosts! It was nothing more than the mind playing tricks. Just guilt, nothing else. A load of bollocks, for certain. His father had done wrong—terrible wrong—and had suffered for it. Fred recalled his father telling him about the nightmares and nervous attacks. How'd he wake up during the night, unable to breathe and soaked with sweat.

Since his had been a deeply troubled life, Charlie's way of coping was to drink. He lost jobs, slept rough—lived from hand to mouth; eventually, he got a good woman, Fred's mother, to marry him. Fred vaguely recalled her. Just a soft voice and gentle hands and tears, too.

He remembered the shouting though—that must have been when Pa told her about the murders. He only did it when he was drunk. Fred was used to seeing his father pissed out of his head. How long ago was that? Donkey's years. Fred smiled at the thought of how he had grown to manhood in America but the old English expressions were still part of him.

His mother cut her own throat. It was awful. There was so much blood, but Fred thought it was paint. He did for years.

"Mum's left us, son. She had to leave."

But what about the paint?

His father hugged him when he asked. "Yes, the paint—she spilled some and left after, see?"

Sure, he saw he was only five but he understood; understood for years. But then when he was sixteen, he found the shoe box with the stuff in it. Bits of china and glass and some brass. His dad caught him handling it and exploded. That was the first time he had hit his son.

Fred sulked for days. His father let him; well, his dad wasn't there. He had left, but not before writing a note where he told him about the murders.

*You have to know, Son. It is important that you do.* That was how it started. He told him, just like that.

Fred didn't remember much after that. He had a kind of collapse and then some hospital treatment. After his father returned, Fred noticed he was changing—growing more vague, more forgetful, until eventually he'd become Old Pa, a blank, sad shell of a man with no memories.

He often thought of his father's brain as being composed of mush. He was certain of that. Poor Old Pa. Yes, he paid for what he did and then some.

If he paid, though, so did Fred. Maybe it wasn't ghosts; maybe it was demons.

\* \* \*

Joe looked really glad to see him. He told him how worried he was about him. "Glad to see you up and around, Fred. See?"

He gestured toward the Midway. Fred nearly gasped. It was really coming to; more lights and everything—signs about Baby Alice and pictures too, done in the old carny freak show drawing style. He loved it.

"We open tomorrow. Can you believe it?"

The smells were just starting up then—all those weird and wild animal smells from the Big Top. There were other smells too, aromas really—of popcorn and cotton candy. The place was jumping!

Joe said the high wire acts were rehearsing and so was Lucy. He smiled when he said that and Fred realized the man knew he liked her. "Go on, go watch!"

She was there alright and Fred watched her. She was good; she could jump up on that running pony like nobody's business. He watched the whole act. On and off, she'd go and do somersaults too, and was she graceful...

Once she was done, she rushed over to him, breathless and beautiful. Her cheeks were flushed and the glow on her face made her even more beautiful. He almost shared that thought with her but restrained himself. Why, he couldn't say.

She told him about the act and how much prepping there was to do. "I follow Bob but he's been right funny today, don't know what it is. Still, it'll be okay on the day, right?"

He assured her it would be. "Let's take a walk..." she said then.

There was something about the pitch of her voice and the look on her face that aroused him.

They walked beyond the encampment toward the woods. She told him things in her soft voice, but he was too excited to listen.

There had been occasions in his life when he came close to marrying but the plans, such as they were, invariably fell through for one reason or another.

Fred always thought the guilt that lived in his heart was the reason. His heart had no room for the love of a woman.

"What do you think?" Her voice cut into his thoughts. "You were a million miles away. Look. Isn't it a beautiful night?"

He looked at the star filled sky. He told her it was beautiful. Then she began to lead him toward a copse of trees. Despite the trees, enough moonlight filtered through for him to see her naked. She had taken her clothing off quickly, and boldly, her eyes never leaving his face. "I want you, Fred. I love you… I've been worried about you."

He told her he was fine. He even smiled to prove it. "I missed you, too…"

Was he in love? Maybe. And maybe everything was going to be alright. He had a woman now, a fine looking young woman who was not ashamed to love him. She wasn't a forward whore who nearly sucked his dick off; she was a talented trick rider. And she loved him. Wasn't it obvious?

They made love there that night in those woods—and it took time because they had the time. And when it was over, and they lay in each other's arms, Lucy snuggled up to him and whispered what she'd like him to do to her.

He was only too happy to accommodate her and when they were thus engaged, giving and receiving pleasure, Joe was taking a little girl by the hand and leading her to Bob's hut.

# Chapter 20

Bob wasn't asleep because he hadn't gotten drunk yet. Every night he had to drink more it seemed in order to sleep. Things preyed on his mind. Awful things. Bad memories are like curses brought by demons. He had always thought that. And the fact that he knew he was a wanted man didn't help.

When he heard the knock, he got frightened. He had to prepare himself to see people. It was complicated. Maybe whoever it was would go away. But no, another knock sounded, a firmer one.

He opened the door. He saw the child first. She was about five—no older, pretty with curly red hair. Joe was holding her hand. Bob didn't want to see the look on the other man's face. "How are you, Bob? I was thinking about you..."

"I was just about to go to sleep."

Joe looked at the half empty bottle near the bed and smiled. "The clowns supply you with that 'shine? That's good."

Bob didn't answer him. "Take the kid and fuck off," he said.

Joe acted shocked in a humorous way. "Language, Bob!" The child was starting to yawn. "Oh, she's tired—probably wants a nap. You'll let her nap, won't you? Sure you will. You like company... You can tell her a story, too, about the bogeyman and his trained dogs. You can promise to show her, right? She'd like that. She'd warm up to that, don't you think?" Joe led her into the room. "You can have Bob's bed, honey. He'll tell you about his dog act and a lot of things besides; he likes children, especially little girls."

Bob was speechless. He watched the child climb onto the bed. Joe stood near the door. "It could have been different, Bob. You know it could have been."

"Take your evil and leave!"

"*My* evil! That's rich," Joe said as he closed the door.

Bob would not go near the bed. The child had fallen asleep. He watched her for a few moments. Then he asked God to forgive him. It had been a long time since he had prayed but this request to the Almighty was important. It was going to be his last. Yes, he was certain of it. He wouldn't be Heaven bound, he knew that.

The razor sat beside his shaving cup.

*Might as well.*

Just one swipe across the throat. That would do it. His hand was trembling badly but he was so determined that he cut deeply. This was no time for superficial cuts. This was a one-time only thing!

The sharp, white-hot pain and the fountain of blood—like a burst water main— didn't stop. He was on the floor by then, clutching his throat

When he hit the floor, the child woke. She almost laughed because she thought he was clowning around. But when he started convulsing, she screamed and ran outside.

Her screams brought folks out. As for Bob, he was happy because it was going to end—all of it. No more depravity, no more urges that he couldn't control. No more self-hating. His last thought was horrific though because he thought of Joe.

Everyone heard the screams. The little girl was in hysterics. Alice wanted to go to her, but Lucy moved faster; she and Fred had come running.

People were asking what had happened. One of the workmen said he heard Bob had cut his throat. Lucy started to shake. "Oh my God," she kept saying.

"Why's the little girl there?" Fred asked.

Joe had rushed over with Tommy Foster. "Oh Christ!" he said. "Why'd he do that?"

Tommy wanted to know from Joe where the kid had come from. Joe said he had no idea. Fred was troubled by the whole thing, especially by Joe because he didn't think he looked as shocked as he should have.

Fred was going to say something to Lucy but she was hugging the kid, trying to calm her down. "I'll take her to Mabel..."

Tommy called the cops. Joe went with him.

It was the fuckingest craziest night. Happy kept saying that over and over. The clowns, too. Noble and Danny looked awful; well, their makeup wasn't on and their scarred faces looked even more scarred in the half light of dawn.

"It's bad luck!" Happy said. "Something happening like this the night before our opening. We're fucked!"

Fred wondered if they were. But then again, maybe he didn't.

\* \* \*

Everyone was questioned by two detectives. They knew Tommy and were very respectful. Tommy looked awful. The first light of day had crept in on them by that time.

Fred had a hunch about what had happened, what with the kid there and all. He asked Lucy. "What gives? Why'd he do it?"

Lucy shrugged. Then she gave him a knowing look. "Who knows, maybe..."

He knew what she meant. Not everything had to be spelled out. In a way he felt sorry for the poor bastard but then again, he didn't. One less creep was good.

"I've been around a lot but never knew any, you know..."

Lucy agreed. "And he was such a nice guy... Who'd have thought...?"

"Can't tell about people."

No, not even murderers when they get old and become senile old men, Fred thought.

The cops took the kid, finally. The child said her name was Cissy. "We'll find your folks, eh, Cissy. Don't you worry about that."

Tommy saw them off. As for Joe, he wasn't around. Lucy asked if Joe was alright and Tommy said he was, adding that he was with Mabel. "We want to be with him now; he's had such a nasty shock."

Nasty wasn't the word for it.

The last to leave the encampment that night was Bob Scobie, deader than shit and nearly bloodless.

# Chapter 21

Happy noticed the dancing girls before he left. They were clustered together, probably discussing the grim events of the night. The Dorinda dame was consoling the other three, who were crying.

Happy was alone by that time. Noble and Danny had already left for the hut. He knew they were going to get shit faced. Why didn't he go with them? Stupid.

Just as he turned to go, Dorinda tapped him on the shoulder. She wanted to know if he was alright. That did it. He started to cry. Now, this was a monumental thing. None of the clowns ever showed their emotions, not even to one another.

Dorinda was upset. "Happy, no, please. Let's talk."

He didn't want to. He begged off through a tearful voice. "I can't remember the last time I cried."

That's what he said, but he knew differently. He had cried plenty as a child. He cried with each new cigarette burn and punch or kick. He wore his suffering like a mantle.

He wasn't worse off than his two pals, though. They had all suffered. Happy started to tell her. "There are things in my past…hard to talk about…"

He was too choked to go on. They were sitting by this time near the Midway. The early morning sun shone on him and he turned away. "I don't want you to see my face."

He covered his face with his hands but Dorinda pulled them down. "You have nothing to apologize for. Please."

He cringed when he saw her looking straight at him.

She offered to get coffee. "Now wait here and we'll have a good chat." Happy felt pleased but when she returned with the coffee, he confessed that he nearly ran off.

She said she knew and smiled. "I'd have looked for you."

After a while she began to tell him about her life. It was no can of peaches. "We all suffer...some more than others. Life can be hell."

When she finished, they were both crying. And when he took her hand to kiss it, she sobbed. With fresh tears still streaking their faces, she asked if she could kiss him.

No one had ever kissed him before, not like that.

"Go and sleep, Happy, but tell me your real name and I'll tell you mine."

"Arthur Mundt," he said.

She nodded. "Gladys Lupo." She spoke a little too curtly.

So it wasn't Dorinda, but something in her eyes told him she wasn't being entirely truthful. He chose to ignore that feeling.

They parted then—she to her hut to dress and he to sleep.

He found Noble and Danny snoring away. They had pissed themselves and the hut stunk. He wasn't about to stay there. Happy had a lot of things wrong with him, one of which was eating human flesh, but he didn't like the smell of urine.

He headed for the woods. It was nice there, quiet and hidden away from everything. Well, it had to be because no one knew, except him and the clowns, that Fred and Lucy had fucked like rabbits earlier.

Christ, he had never seen so much screwing! He was glad for the man. Fred was an okay guy. Who else would turn a blind eye to all the shit he and his buddies got up to?

It struck him funny and he laughed to himself. That was when he heard someone call, 'Arthur.' He turned around but he didn't see anyone.

He decided to explore the woods a little. And so he stepped up a little hill and found, to his delight, a pond! He wondered if anyone knew it was there.

As he made his way toward it, he realized a woman was swimming, her body gliding through the water in long graceful strokes. He watched fascinated as she stood up. He'd never seen a body like that, her breasts as beautiful and inviting as the thatch of black pubic hair.

Instead of covering herself, she laughed. "Arthur! Come in, it's delicious."

He tried to move fast but it wasn't easy. He didn't want her to see his erection. It was massive too. "I'll stay here," he said.

She offered to turn around. "I won't look!"

"Okay!" he cried as he hurried toward her, tearing his clothes off.

She didn't turn, not until he tapped her on the shoulder. She saw it in the water. "I didn't realize you were so big!"

He laughed but he was proud. It was the only thing he was proud of—not that he got to use it much. Not like Danny and Noble. Of course, he knew most of what they said was wishful thinking.

She pulled him close, and they started doing it right there. Her lovemaking went beyond his wildest expectations. She was skilled; she could bring him off gently. He had never known anything like it.

She led him from the water. And he followed, proudly. She began touching him when they lay down. Her touch was magic, her lips a soft caress.

She told him all kinds of things. Things she wanted him to do. He did them and more, besides.

He tried to be gentle but his passion got the better of him a few times. She told him she was fine when he asked if he had hurt her.

"No," she whispered.

He couldn't believe how long he lasted. Nor could he fathom how satisfied he had made her. And when they both climaxed, it was like they were one, shuddering mass.

She wrapped him in a towel and dried him off—then herself, giggling as she did because she paid very special attention to his penis.

"It's resting now," he joked. Her laughter carried like music to his ears.

They lay together for the longest time, both falling asleep.

While he was sleeping, she rose and stretched and then flew over the pond and back again. He never caught sight of that or her massive wings.

She was by his side when he woke up and he was comforted. "I want you now," she said. He soon saw just how much she did.

# Chapter 22

It had been a tough day. Alice was upset about Bob's suicide. Al tried to calm her down, by making love to her. She was pretty hot, usually ready for a good screw. And since she slept especially well after one, he wanted to please her. He did all the usual stuff because it wasn't easy to get the damned thing accomplished.

"It's okay," Alice said. "We're both tired." She kissed him good night and went to sleep. He was relieved when he heard her snore, and then fell asleep. Her crying woke him. She cried sometimes in her sleep.

"Shut up, will ya? Christ, I tried, didn't I?"

Okay, he thought. Better try again, not that it was easy. It was getting a lot harder to find the appropriate place to stick his ding dong in. Her front was impossible and approaching from the back, the usual target area was also proving more and more difficult.

They took their usual positions; him in back and her trying to maneuver herself so he'd be successful. In the early days of their relationship, it had proved easier, but she was less fat then.

Finally, he pushed her aside and told her he was going to have a cigarette. She started to cry.

"You don't love me anymore," she said.

"Look, just 'cause I find it hard to fuck you doesn't mean I don't love you. Course I do. You're my fiancée, ain't ya?"

He tweaked one huge tit and lit a cigarette at the same time.

She didn't answer him, which meant she was pissed off. He did have feelings for her; not that they were as deep as previously, but he did like her. He certainly didn't want to hurt her feelings. And he did want to marry her or at least, he told himself he did.

"I'm going to sleep now," she said. She had put on her wrap, too, just to show him she didn't want any love making. "You can sleep in your own bed. I don't mind."

He did have a little cot he liked to sleep in. Well, for Christ sakes, sleeping next to someone the size of Alice wasn't easy. He had, in the early part of their relationship, been worried she'd crush him if she ever rolled over on him.

But he went for it because he did want to make her happy. "Alice…"

She giggled. "Well, alright then."

He tried so hard, touching whatever he could reach. She trembled and he smiled with relief at the quickness of her pleasure. She always said he had magic fingers.

When he heard her snoring again, he went to sleep. But then she must have had one of her nightmares. She'd had them ever since he knew her. Any time he asked her about them, she would say it was all due to her awful beginnings.

"Goddamn it Alice, what did you dream this time?"

She wouldn't tell him at first; she kept shaking her head. But then, she finally said, "Okay! I killed my fucking father, alright?"

Al started to laugh. "Big deal. He deserved it. Why, Hank and I…"

"I ate his fucking eyes!"

That stopped him cold. He had never liked that particular proclivity of the clowns—eating human flesh—so he was shocked.

"I just pulled them out of his head and ate them, first one and then the other. He wasn't even dead yet."

They stared at one another for some time. Al almost threw up, which was really something. Finally, he got hold of himself. "Your hate did that… I hated people that I killed. So did Hank, and you know about the clowns."

She nodded. From the look in her eyes, he realized she wanted something. "I need a hug," she said.

Al would have laughed if he hadn't been so repulsed by the cannibalism. She opened her wrap as if to entice him. "You don't have to do anything."

Because she winked, he knew what she meant. She'd get him off—not something she usually did. He didn't want it though. It had reached the point where he couldn't stand her touch—hands or mouth. *That mouth that ate flesh.*

"Fuck you!" he said, before slamming the door.

\* \* \*

She began to cry. The humiliation was fierce. Not only had he rebuffed her, he had done it when she'd bared her soul to him. Gave him her heartfelt confession!

She was still crying when she heard a soft knock. "Al?" Was he back?! "Come in, Petal! Come to Mama!" she called.

The door opened but it wasn't Al. Joe and Hank walked in. She couldn't close her wrap fast enough.

"Aren't you going to invite us in? We have something for you."

"Sure, come in. Excuse me."

Joe smiled. "You don't have to excuse yourself. I am sorry we embarrassed you, but I must say you are beautiful." Alice shook her head. "No really," he insisted. "You are lovely. Big and beautiful. Lots of men like women that way, right, Hank?"

Hank nodded eagerly but his smile looked fixed.

"Anyway, we have something for you. Thought you might like it. Cook had a special dinner to welcome the master of ceremonies. You haven't met him yet, have you?"

Alice didn't care about that; she was staring at the covered plate.

Joe whipped the napkin off. "It's a very special stew. It's good; you can have it if you like."

Sure, why not? It smelled so good. She couldn't wait. She thanked them and watched them go. It had the most wonderful aroma. Alice loved food, that was obvious—but mostly she just stuffed her mouth, without really enjoying what she ate.

The first bite just about melted in her mouth. The meat was tender. Lamb, perhaps? Whatever it was, it tasted heavenly. For a woman her size, Alice was generally a dainty eater, but this dish proved so fantastic that she just gobbled it up, shoving handfuls into her mouth and moaning while she did.

It was better than sex and because of that, she didn't give a flying fuck when her little man came back. In fact, she wasn't even thinking of him. Suddenly, she felt the most intense hunger, as well as thirst.

She knew there was nothing to drink. Her eyes began to scan the hut. There had to be something…

When she saw the mouse, she cried out. Somehow, she was able to grab it. It only struggled for a second. That was all the time it took for her to bite its head off. She drained it and then ate it.

Then she caught a glimpse of herself in the mirror, the mouse blood stained all over her chin and breast. Well, not both, but one got a bit splattered. And because she liked what she saw, she smiled.

\* \* \*

Hank and Joe watched her from outside and giggled to themselves. Damned if she didn't always fly back with the best stuff. But then again, children's flesh was always to be prized.

"Never figured her for a blood sucker," Joe said. "Still, you never know about people."

"Was it because you blessed the food, Joe?"

Joe didn't answer; he only winked.

# Chapter 23

Noble and Danny were jealous because Happy didn't spare one detail about his love making. They got so tired of hearing about his massive erection, they started to deliberately yawn.

Happy wasn't Happy. "For God sakes, fellas! It's been a long time."

"Yeah and for me, too!"

Noble tittered. "But in your case, eating doesn't really mean eating."

"I never ate no one I fucked!"

"Oh yes, you did. You ate at least three women I know about. As in *eating*, eating!"

Happy was furious. "Did not!"

Danny agreed. "Really, brother—remember that hooker we shared in Denver? The one with the red hair? After you ate her, you *ate* her! You told us to join in but we didn't. You couldn't even stop. It was a mess!"

Happy was rapidly getting more pissed off by the second. "No, you preferred to kill a newsboy instead."

"Two actually," Danny admitted. "Nasty little bastards, they had it coming! It's not like we usually do kids."

That Happy liked. "Precisely. That is why I had no desire to eat Dorinda afterwards...or during..."

"We get the picture."

They did, too. And it struck them funny. When they laughed, Happy joined in because he hated for his friends to be angry with him.

*Circus of Horrors*

After sharing some of their goriest adventures, they decided to relax. They still had the French postcards Noble bought once. Those were well-thumbed. Each postcard (there were thirty) had been discussed time and again. Still, they always found they could think of more things to ask one another.

"Danny," Noble asked. "How do they get them girls to pose like that?"

"They're pros. You know—whores. Whores don't care who sees what they have."

Danny agreed. "Let me see your ten now. I'm tired of mine."

They switched. Happy wasn't interested. He was thinking of Dorinda.

When he heard her call from outside, he almost fainted. "Ditch them cards," he said as he rushed to open the door. Boy, was he thrilled to see her.

"I just wanted to ask you guys if you'd like to see a rehearsal. We open tomorrow and me and the girls have a special act we'd like you to see."

The clowns never moved faster. Dorinda pointed to a tent on the Midway. "That's it."

It was a good-sized tent with lots of signs and pictures showing the dancing girls, each scantily dressed. The classic sign read: "For 10 cents you will see the secrets of the Orient! Feast your eyes on the Sultan's pleasure!"

The clowns liked that and Dorinda smiled. "This way, fellas."

They didn't have to wait long. She clapped her hands and the girls appeared, one by one. Exotic music strains sounded from a Victrola.

The girls' costumes were colorful but not too revealing, which disappointed the fellas. But they looked good dressed like Arabian belly dancers. Dorinda took them through the whole routine.

"Now this is the dance we will all do."

Dorinda joined them, without her dress, just in her undies. Happy and the boys loved it. But when they all stripped off and started to dance naked as jay birds, the clowns nearly died.

They danced around like that, as seductive and beguiling as they could be. When the music reached a crescendo, they draped themselves over their audience. The boys didn't waste any time. Noble had the blonde and Danny the brunette. As for Happy, he looked at Dorinda as if to ask for permission. She nodded, so he started with the redhead.

She knew what she wanted. "Harder, honey. Yeah, just like that."

The orgy started when they all changed partners and Dorinda joined in. She took all three clowns at the same time, paying special attention to Happy.

None of them had ever been to an orgy but Dorinda explained they were fun—and why the fuck not have fun when you can? Lucky no one was around because the session lasted for hours, what with the partner changes and different positions.

When it ended, the guys were sleepy as hell, as well as drunk. They never saw Dorinda and the girls leave or fly off—nor did they see them come back carrying children. The first they knew about it was when Dorinda showed them their booty.

Happy and his pals were appalled. "What? To eat them, you mean?"

"But they're dead. They won't feel it. Besides, you've eaten flesh before..." Dorinda couldn't understand the problem.

Happy asked them to leave. This they were not about to do. Dorinda smiled and began to sing. As she did, the boys started to cry, for they had never heard such a sound in their lives. Her voice carried to them like magic. All of the pain of their entire lives began to be eased away.

Happy was about to say something, to ask her about the song, when the other three started to sing. They sang together and harmonized beautifully.

Noble wept and Danny removed his clown makeup. When his face was bare, one of the dancers went over to him to kiss him, but she did more than that—she began to lick his face. All those scars and ruts, she licked and kissed. He cried out for he was ashamed of them. "No, please!"

But she only laughed, and licked his face some more.

Dorinda did Happy's face. He was embarrassed about the tears but she didn't care.

When all three clowns had their faces clean, they lay down to sleep. The sirens, for that is what they really were, had begun singing again. Then, when the boys slept, they smiled and spoke quietly. It was all about their purpose and if that wasn't wonderful, it was about pleasure, too.

Dorinda pulled the other sirens close to her and they giggled and touched one another. And while they did this, they began to change—from women with beautiful hair and fine bodies they changed into men, then into animals and birds. They could do this because they had never been human.

They loved the changing, as they called it. In each form, they explored different ways of pleasuring one another. This transforming and pleasuring lasted for hours and still, the clowns slept.

The clowns woke to seeing the sirens looking as the dancers they knew. "Eat, my love, eat," they coaxed. This they said as each held a handful of the food they had brought to them. Happy smiled for he no longer cared what he was given. He opened his mouth and ate, savoring the taste.

Each followed his example. Noble and Danny ate and all the while, the dancers sang. There was joy in the songs—joy and promises of a darkness none of the clowns could imagine.

"*You will have bounty after bounty—nothing shall be wrong... no act despised, no desire denied,*" Dorinda sang.

She led them out afterwards. "We shall take you places you have never dreamed of..."

Each of them took one of the clowns and flew off. Only Dorinda remained behind but that was in order to visit Fred.

\* \* \*

He was asleep when the succubus began to pleasure him. This time, he did not waken. This time, he just slept on, enjoying her touch and all that she was doing to him.

His father finally looked over. It was Fred's cries of ecstasy that drew his attention. But, being senile, Charley didn't think anything of the naked woman—nor did he even notice when she turned into a man. Had he any of his senses, he'd have recognized Joe.

# Chapter 24

Fred was surprised to see Mabel. He needed to wash up—that fucking wet dream again! Old Pa was just having a good old bowel movement on the chamber pot too when Mabel poked her head in. Fred apologized.

Mabel waved him off. "I take people as I find them," she said.

Then she explained why she was there. "Fred, I think your people listen to you better than they listen to me. I am depending on you to get them all ready by four. The show starts at six. I also have something else I'd like to discuss with you."

Fred had never seen her looking so attractive. The white dress danced along her curves. He tried not to look at the dark spot showing through between her legs. Could it be she wasn't wearing knickers?

And if that wasn't enough to throw him, he tried to avoid looking at her nipples because they were sure sticking out of her dress. She didn't seem to notice his discomfort and he was pleased.

"Let me tell you why I'm here. I thought you'd like to work spare time in the souvenir stand we're building. We're going to sell toys and trinkets to the folks. Tommy's idea—and Joe thinks it's a good one."

She stepped up to him and he got a good whiff of her perfume. "I best be going so you can finish with your dad. By the way, I can have someone stay with him later if you like because Lester is busy now. I'll send a man around. How's that?"

Fred was very grateful.

He watched her leave. And he cried because he was ashamed of the stink and how he felt. So many things were getting on top of him—the place felt wrong, starting with Joe. But he had his father to care for, so he wasn't going to leave. He reasoned he might eventually get round to it, but not now. Now he was going to make sure his people were ready for the opening.

He went to see Al but he wasn't with Alice. "I don't know where that little fucker is. Him and me, we broke up," she said. Opening her wrap, she lifted up an enormous boob. "Oh look, I got blood on my tit. Want to lick it off?"

Fred was in shock. He had never heard her speak that way. Her voice sounded funny and her eyes looked crazy. She was polite but her face was flushed and her mouth looked all bloody.

Fred was worried. "Are you alright? Did you hurt your gums or something?"

She wiped her mouth and laughed, and when she saw the blood on her hand, she nodded. "Oh yeah. I scratched it or something in my sleep." She looked at him then. "I can't stand Al, actually. I want to feel a man inside me. His dick is like my pinkie!" She held up her fat pinkie and wiggled it. "Can you imagine anyone getting their rocks off with something this size? Let me see your dick. I've never seen it. Is it big?"

Fred couldn't get out of there fast enough. He said he had to go.

"Sure, but why not come back later?" she said. She poked her head out of the door, blocking his way. "He's got himself another dame. Joe brought her over yesterday. He said the men pay extra 'cause her twat's so little."

By this time, Fred wanted to run. "By the way," she called. "Don't be a stranger!"

Fred got a whiff of something putrid then. The smell of blood and something else. He didn't know how but there were several partially eaten corpses under the bed. Some were animals and some weren't. All of them were hollowed out because Alice had eaten all of their insides. She giggled to herself as she reached under her pillow for the private parts she had put there.

\* \* \*

Fred found Al in his old hut. He was naked but for a towel wrapped around his waist. A beautiful little woman stood behind him. When she came forward, Fred could see she was a midget—the one Alice had been talking about.

"This is Darla," Al said. "Ain't she sweet? I met her last night. Joe introduced us. She's new to the circus. We're going to have our own act."

"But what about Hank?"

Al shook his head and smiled. "Hank doesn't mind. He knows. He's Joe's assistant in everything. Joe says he's an official and will be treated as such! Ain't that great?"

Darla squealed with delight.

Fred was pleased in a way but doubtful, too—if things had struck him as strange before, it was worse now by a hundred fold. But he could be wrong, so he asked about the new act.

"Well, we're going to be called Mr. and Mrs. Small and they'll say we're married. Dexter will lift us up, like he was going to do with me and Hank. Joe says we'll marry sometime for real in front of an audience. Then we'll honeymoon, too." He winked. "I sure ain't engaged to that fucking cow anymore! No, sir!" Al put his arm around Darla. "She's little but she's got all the stuff in the right places. Say girl, how many times did you have me come?"

Darla giggled but didn't answer.

"And Hank's alright about it?"

Al didn't answer. He was too busy kissing Darla.

\* \* \*

Hank looked happy. Fred didn't ever remember seeing him this happy as the man ran toward him. "Fred! Fred did you hear about Joe's idea of the souvenir stand? I think it's great."

"Sounds interesting. When's it supposed to open?"

"Tomorrow! Too bad it couldn't be for later—the official opening. But Joe thought of it late, see? They're just building the stand now. Want to see?"

Fred let the little man lead him over to the tent. It was one of those open tents. Workmen about, and a counter had already been installed.

"See, the items for sale will go in this display case. Wow, have you ever seen anything like it?"

Fred had a zillion times but he said he hadn't.

"You know what the best part about it is, Fred? I'm going to be your assistant! Me! Can you believe it?"

Fred was pleased for Hank but now the things that troubled him seemed to be multiplying, growing more and more like something festering.

# Chapter 25

He found his father looking comfortable. The man with him was polite. "Your father is a nice old fella. Any time you need me… just ask for Andy." He gave Fred a searching look, then added, "You mind a question?"

Fred said he didn't mind.

"How do you like it here? I've been here only a few days and I don't know…"

"I sometimes don't know either. Can't put my finger on it." Fred shrugged. "It just feels wrong sometimes."

They discussed the feeling of wrongness for a few minutes.

"Miss Mabel offered me a job. She said I looked tired. I was and hungry, too. She seemed very nice. 'It must be worse for you…' she said. I felt funny when she said that 'cause she meant my color… but I agreed. I said there were two kinds of poor: white poor and colored poor. I took her up on the job offer."

"But you wish you hadn't."

"Man, do I ever. I'm going to leave next week—wait till I get paid, though. Don't trust no one." He flashed Fred a sad smile and left.

Fred watched him walk away and went to sit by his father. "Nice man, isn't he, Pa? Too nice for here, I reckon. Perhaps it's time to move on…"

Old Pa had been smiling his bland, dopey smile when he suddenly started to get strange. He grabbed a hold of Fred and started shaking.

"What is it, Pa? Why are you upset?"

Old Pa looked hard at him. "Can't."

"Can't, what?"

His father put his finger to his lips as if to silence him or himself. All Fred could do was wonder what upset his father. "You like it here...?"

Old Pa put his fingers to his lips again, only this time he spoke. He managed an entire sentence: "Can't leave. They'll know..."

"Know what?"

It was useless for whatever brief flicker of coherence had been his father's, it was gone now. Fred didn't know what to think, or maybe he did.

Maybe he'd plan on leaving sometime. The question was, where would they go? He'd have his pickup but that was it—that and his senile, old father. And he wasn't getting any younger. He considered what he had and what he'd have to go through and all that could happen. Finally, he came to the conclusion that he didn't have the guts to leave. He'd have to stay. Maybe things would get better.

\* \* \*

If he were going to remain, he'd have to stop questioning things like reality. Not an easy thing to do because his brain still worked. He did often feel he was losing his power to reason though. He had begun to wonder if he was becoming insane. In a way, he hoped he was. Of course, he didn't want to end up in a nut ward somewhere. The idea of being out of it in some way did appeal though: having his decisions made possibly by a loving Lucy who would care both for him and Old Pa. Now that might not be hard to take.

In order to achieve all of that, he decided not to be argumentative. If he had questioned where all the animals and circus stuff came from previously, he thought he'd be better off now not to question anything.

Yeah, but how long that would last?

\* \* \*

The Big Top was buzzing. He heard the loud growls of the lions and tigers as well as the crack of the whip and the shouted commands of the handler. They were beautiful animals but they scared the shit out of him.

Queenie the elephant was another story; she was a gentle giant. All dressed up with a different colored headband each time he saw her. Her handler told Fred the elephant is considered sacred to the Hindu. "She is my friend," he said. "And a good one."

Another man had replaced Bob—young and good-looking. Fred didn't think anything of it until he saw Lucy flirting with him. He greeted her a little loudly. She looked thrilled to see him. "This is Tombo," she said. "Tombo comes from Spain, don't you?"

Said Tombo had to be six foot four, easy. Handsome and broad shouldered, with a big fucking bulge the size of Detroit between his legs. Jealousy gripped Fred.

Imelda, the trapeze star, was saying all kinds of shit to Tombo, and her husband looked like if she kept it up, he might just not catch her right the next time they flew.

Fred turned away before anyone recognized him. He didn't want to speak to any of them. He only wanted to see Lucy.

\* \* \*

The circus opened right on time. The officials—including the mayor and his wife, were present. At first, Fred didn't know who they were, but they seemed to be enjoying Joe's company.

Circus music sounded from a band. Fred wondered when they had been hired. It was a good idea, whoever thought of it. All kinds of folks poured in and he started to feel excited. It was like old times. He thought of all the different shows he had been in or part of.

There were lots of families with kids; most poorly dressed yokels with wide eyes and hardly any money to spend. Fred knew that at once. He had seen enough of them to know.

So why the souvenir stand? Would it really make money? Maybe it would; you can't figure folk. Some things you think will be successful aren't and vice versa. Besides, so few people had money to spend.

Of course, Tommy seemed to know what was what and Joe acted as though he certainly did.

\* \* \*

The Midway looked swell all lit up. It was filling up fast, too. The dancing girls had drawn a lot of attention, especially from a cluster of men who watched them. Their women looked to be in a huff; most had begun walking away.

Dorinda, the lead dancer, had her girls shimmy like crazy. Fred wondered if there would be complaints. There usually would be from church group types, especially the women.

Lester and Don were wowing the crowd, as well as The Wildman and Gorilla Lady. Poor woman was dressed up and as hairy as hell. She only laughed and waved people off as they shouted at her.

Alice sat on her throne, looking as though she didn't give a fuck. She had some hecklers but she'd just grin at them. Fred wondered why her teeth looked red. *Better ask about a dentist.*

Dexter, the muscle man, seemed okay. He told Fred the little couple were sweet as pie. "First midgets I ever worked with," he said. He added that he had some tough times working circuses. "Not everyone is as nice as these folks…"

Fred didn't say anything because the act was starting. He watched as Dexter held up Al and Darla. The crowd loved it. They looked cute, too, all dressed up in evening clothes. Fred wondered where they came from. Joe, probably.

The clowns were milling around, laughing and waving to the children. Happy waved to every pretty girl he saw. He whispered too, which made Fred tense up. But the girls didn't look shocked. Thank God for that.

Happy greeted him and said how great it all was. Fred agreed. The clowns crowded around him, then and they all headed for the Big Top.

The tent was filled to capacity. Every spot on the bleachers was taken. "It's a good night," Fred murmured.

The crowd got quiet when the ringmaster entered. Buck Carson. Fred had met him years before. Tommy probably plucked him from whatever show he was with. Hell of a thing about Buck. He had a barrel chest and a deep voice. No one had any idea he liked dressing up like a little girl. Fred had seen him mincing around many encampments. Circus folks are tolerant and people laughed, but Fred thought he was nuts.

"Ladies and gentlemen, children of all ages..."

The spiel that never fails began as each act was introduced. The acts ran smoothly. Imelda and Ramon wowed them although it seemed to Fred, Ramon made Imelda sweat out his catching her. No doubt payback for her flirting with Tombo.

And Tombo! He was great, better than Bob had ever been. Lucy was at her best and the two eventually switched places—he did the pony trick riding and she took over the dogs. That nearly brought down the house. People cheered and stomped.

She looked beautiful up there—never lovelier. He had such an urge to talk to her. Eventually, he left to wait for her at her hut.

So he never saw the clowns sniffing the audience. Nor did he see them deciding who they were going to eat.

# Chapter 26

He couldn't wait to see Lucy. At last, she appeared. She greeted him warmly but when he said he had to talk to her, she begged off. "I only have an hour before the next show. Just enough time to change and freshen up."

"Can I see you later?"

She looked perplexed. "Anything wrong…your father…?"

"No, nothing like that. It's just… I wanted to speak to you."

She took his hand and squeezed it. "Anything for you, Fred. Come by after midnight. I'll be waiting!"

\* \* \*

The last two people Fred wanted to see greeted him. Joe and Hank looked like they owned the fucking place.

"How's it hangin'?" Joe asked.

Fred didn't answer. Fuck him.

Joe was studying him. Whenever he did, Fred felt like squirming. It was hard not to look relaxed.

Joe suggested they walk and talk. "So what do you think about the souvenir stand?"

"Don't know. Times… being what they are…"

Joe waved him off. "Yeah, but there's always kids nagging their folks for a doll or a toy. They'll drag them! Don't you think?"

Fred shrugged. "How the hell do I know?"

Hank started to laugh. "Come on, Fred. Don't be grumpy."

"Yeah, Fred—don't be a grumpy."

Fred didn't feel like decking Hank, but he'd have loved to bloody Joe's nose.

Still, he followed them to the stand. He was surprised at how it looked. "Where'd all the stock come from so fast?"

"We were lucky about that. There was a dealer that came around and damned if he didn't have almost everything we needed." Joe showed off the stuff.

Fred's eyes swept over it. Dolls everywhere, baby dolls and cutsie dolls, even soldier dolls. And as for monkeys, they were really something.

"Cute, huh? Watch this!" Joe wound up one and the little monkey toy started to play its drum.

"Yeah, cute." Fred didn't give two shits about it, but thought it best to sound positive. "Should sell some…"

"Glad you feel that way. Hank is excited, too. Ain't ya, Hank?"

Hank agreed. "Can't wait."

"The stand opens noon tomorrow and stays open till eleven. You guys will relieve each other for breaks and meals. Tommy, don't overwork anyone. I'll stay here and make sure nothing gets swiped. Not everyone's honest. Hank, you go and talk to Fred."

Fred and Hank went off together, with Fred wondering what the little guy was going to talk about. He started off right away. "Joe's been wondering about your dad, Fred. How is everything?"

"Oh, fine. He's okay—he's old and getting older… It's hard sometimes, that's all…"

Why'd Joe ask about Old Pa? *Creepy.*

They were standing near the Midway when Hank suggested they go in for a drink, so they did. He began to speak then about how long they had known one another and how Fred's friendship meant so much to him. Then he changed topic. "It seems," he said, "Al's got himself another dame."

Fred spoke about Darla and how happy they seemed and Hank nodded sadly.

"Yeah, I seen her with him. They do look pretty happy, I'll grant you... I don't know—whatever is happening, I just don't think Al is my friend anymore."

Fred felt sorry for the little man. "People change sometimes, Hank."

"I got Joe now, he's my friend. We're very close. I can tell him anything. Joe's a special person. He really cares about all of us. And he sure knows the business alright."

They spoke what Fred considered to be a lot of horseshit after that. Hank didn't shut up, either. He kept going on about Joe's gifts of friendship and how caring he was. "Take your dad," Hank said. "Joe really is concerned about him. He wants you to know that... see, he don't want any of his people to be upset."

*His* people?

"Joe wants you to open yourself to him. He thinks you hate him."

Now began a litany of all of Joe's many attributes told from Hank's point of view. In many ways, Fred could understand it. Hank had suffered so much throughout his life and had been recently dumped by his best buddy. Sure, he longed for friendship or perhaps something more. Still, Fred didn't understand the ardency in Hank's expression or the glow in his eyes. It seemed as though he had found religion or something. "You really like him."

"I adore him. He is so much to me..." Hank's voice trailed off because he was too choked up to speak.

\* \* \*

The clowns had zeroed in on a fat man. Fat and slow and stupid. He had come alone. There he was, walking down the Midway, all eyes—eating his hot dogs.

Happy couldn't get over the various aromas. The hot dogs and the man himself, his hair oil, and his flesh.

Noble said he thought the guy smelled of beer, too. Danny laughed. "Okay by me because I like beer."

They hadn't done anything like this before—like they were planning to do. They had only eaten people they killed and they only killed those that had hurt or insulted them or their friends, but this was different. This was something else, a new feeling. Something predatory had seized hold of them.

They followed the guy to the end of the Midway. When they realized they were alone, they called to him. Happy joked around with him, distracting him. Then Noble and Danny knocked him out.

"The woods. No one is there now."

Danny wanted to know if they'd have a fire. He had never eaten anyone raw before.

Happy laughed as he took out his straight razor and cut the man's throat. They stood over the poor jerk, watching him convulse as he bled to death.

"See, it's over fast. Who wants what?"

Noble said he'd take anything. When Danny didn't answer, Happy chided him. "Stop being so fussy. This is a new experience for us," he said removing the man's eyeballs. "Here, try one."

Danny hesitated but with enough urging, he took the offering. A shadow had passed over the moon then and a sudden wind blew up just when he bit into the eye. "Yeah, it's good. Just like hard boiled eggs," he said.

## Chapter 27

Lucy was waiting for him. Now that he was with her, he didn't know what to say. He had wanted to confide his darkest fears to her, what he thought about Joe and the whole damned circus, but for some reason, he didn't have the gumption.

She had on a dressing gown. He knew she was naked under it.

"Have a drink. It'll relax you."

"I'm okay."

When she got up to pour the drink, her gown opened and he saw her nakedness. "Oh! Pardon me," she said.

But her tone implied she was glad he saw her. He took the drink from her without question. Maybe it would be good to get drunk. He wouldn't worry so much or be scared.

She watched him swallow it down. It was warm and good and he smiled because he was feeling especially relaxed. He felt alert but different, more content. Whatever was bothering him had faded away. The only thing on his mind was Lucy.

He watched her slip out of her gown. "It's you I care about, Fred. I just do. You know that."

They didn't speak much; in fact, that was the only conversation they had other than what Lucy said she wanted him to do to her. He obeyed happily. And when he was finished, she said, "Now, relax..." And he complied, as she did all the work.

Both offered proclamations of undying love—sweet and moving. And it helped; boy, did it ever.

He kissed her long and hard. "I love you, Lucy... I always will."

They kissed again and he left.

He had no idea Dorinda had come out from under the bed, nor did he know she was his regular succubus. Both Dorinda and Lucy giggled about it, that and the special drink Fred had taken. Then they kissed. In a moment, they were doing it too—whatever they could do as women. Then, when they both began to change into men and after that, into various animals, they continued to copulate however such creatures were wont to do.

The last transformation occurred when Lucy turned into a great winged creature and flew outside with Dorinda accompanying her.

\* \* \*

The clowns had eaten most of the fat man but certain parts, they didn't want. No one wanted the sexual organs, although Noble did taste them. "I never liked those sorts of things."

"Yeah," Happy said. "But you should try different things."

Noble agreed. "True, but I still prefer buttocks and eye balls."

They all did.

"So what do we do with him now?"

Redundant question. They had to bury what was left. But where?

Happy suggested wrapping him up in a blanket (which Noble went for) and burying him. "He deserves a shroud of some kind," he said.

They did this, and buried him quickly in a shallow grave. "Hope those fucking dogs don't dig him up..."

When they headed back to their hut to sleep, they met Joe. "Hi fellas, you guys busy?"

Happy liked Joe but he had the funniest feeling he knew what they had done. Was it possible he had seen them?

He didn't ask them anything, just spoke about the first day—and how it all went so well "Don't you think so?" he asked them. They all agreed, each embellishing on the other's observation. Now they were all three worried.

"Look boys, I want to talk to you about something. What do you say we speak in my hut?"

They found Hank naked in bed. As there was only one bed, the clowns knew and they smiled. "Hi Hank, how's it going?"

Hank, who hadn't been teased in a long time, smiled stiffly and got up. They caught a flash of his dick and had to keep from laughing. It was just like a baby's.

"Hank, why don't you get dressed and get us some coffee from the commissary?" Joe asked. The boys turned away so as to give him some privacy. When he was gone, Joe began.

"You are my friends, boys. We all work for Tommy but we're all friends here. I hope you feel as I do."

"Sure we do!"

"Good." Joe smiled. "I want to be able to feel I can trust you. See, some people are trouble—that is, they could bring trouble down on us. I've made an enemy or two along the way. Old carnies that I didn't get on with. If any show up, it'll be to attack and kill me. It's just how it is. Tommy's men know and they are great and will help me. But you never know when I might need your services."

Services—that sounded interesting. They all liked that because it made them feel proud.

Joe took a telegram out of his pocket. "This came for me, Western Union. I'll read it to you."

"Joe, it's not over. Your words not mine. Expect me when you see me."

"That's a threat!" Happy shouted. "Sure is," they all agreed, then assured their mentor and friend, "Don't worry. We'll take care of it for you."

Joe's eyes filled with tears. The sight moved them. He embraced each one. "Your friendship and loyalty mean everything to me," he said. "I can relax now."

# Chapter 28

Fred thanked Andy when he came back. He was relieved to see his father asleep.

"I put him down at eight. He was worn out. He done shit and peed first though, so you should be okay."

Fred had the feeling Andy wanted to tell him something. "You can tell me anything, really," he said.

"Well, it's like this. Like I said, it's not easy to get a steady job nowadays and so I stay and overlook things I might not overlook normally. Mrs. Foster has always been polite to me and her husband fair. But she did show me herself once... That frightened me and I try to avoid her."

Fred understood. "I know what you mean. I was thinking about leaving. I guess, putting it off really. But maybe we'll leave, too, Old Pa and I. We'll discuss it soon. We can't just rush into anything."

Andy looked pleased. They bid each other good night and Fred closed the door. *So she's a flasher...* That accounted for the clothes she wore; she *was* a fucking tease.

He thought of Lucy then, got a flash of her naked. Images of her lying on the bed, telling him to fuck her... Funny because he couldn't remember if that had been real or not. He had no memory of their last encounter.

Something was bothering him about her but he couldn't remember what it was. One thought led to another and he lay back in his bed, wondering if that fucking crazy dream would happen again. But there were other things he wondered as well, other worries he had. Still, he fell into a sound sleep.

\* \* \*

The clowns saw them when they arrived. Hank came to alert them. "Them guys that Joe said was coming for him are here. They're questioning Joe in his hut. Two detectives and a third guy. Not sure who he is. I seen 'em and so I came for you."

They headed right over there. They could hear loud talking, shouting really. Joe was trying to explain something.

The clowns knocked on the door. A cop answered. Had to be, with his suit and hat pulled down low. "Yeah, whaddya want?"

Joe waved and nodded. His signal, they knew. When the other cop stood, they were able to see the third man. He was thin and old looking, with a wiry frame. He turned to look at them. "These your friends?" he asked Joe.

"They certainly are," he answered. The tone of his voice made the clowns each feel good.

Happy smiled. "Whatever your beef is, why don't you scram?"

"He won't never scram," Joe said. "Will you, Monty? He even brought the law here."

Monty looked scared but angry, too. "Your days of terrorizing folk are over, you crazy bastard. Your employee has to answer for the child molestations. Where is he?"

"He's dead. Killed himself. Go check."

"You're protecting him!"

"I'm not!"

The man wasn't having it. "They were my granddaughters, you fucking bastard!" This he said as he whipped out a razor.

The cops took it off him.

"This bastard," he said, gesturing toward Joe, "is evil, just plain evil! Ask him, why don't you, about all the people he's killed! Cause he has!"

*Circus of Horrors*

The clowns moved to attack the man just as the cops went for their guns. They never got them out. The clowns cut their throats. When the man started to plead with them, Joe smiled and nodded—another signal.

Happy slit the old geezer's throat so deeply, he nearly took his head off. The place was a mess of blood, evacuated bowels and urine. The clowns offered to clean it up.

"You go and relax, Joe. Noble, you go with him and see that he does. Danny and I will clean this place up. As for the stiffs, we'll put them in our hut to deal with later," Happy added.

Noble knew what that meant and snorted a laugh.

\* \* \*

It was Fred's first day at the stand. Hank was so excited, he kept rubbing his hands. "What do you think?"

"Looks good. Fully stocked, I see."

"There'll be more stuff later or tomorrow. Actually, Joe tells me we'll be upping the inventory regularly."

Fred wondered about that but then figured things must depend on how the merchandise moved. Before he had a chance to say anything else, some people came in, couples with kids. The little girls went wild over the dolls. But the boys loved the monkey.

They pleaded a lot and the parents smiled and teased them. Fred saw they weren't poor. Their clothes were nice and the lady's hair was all marcelled and fancied up.

Fred and the husband talked about the circus and the woman asked Hank about the shows. "It's just wonderful! The children love the elephant and the pony rider especially. Don't you, children?"

They looked like nice kids. Two girls and a boy. They agreed shyly but their eyes were fixed on what they wanted. That was obvious.

The woman began to giggle. "Alright. Why don't you each pick a toy that you'd like?"

They did. The girls picked two dolls and the boy the monkey with the drum. Hank wound it up and the little boy laughed.

It wasn't until the family left with their purchases that Hank sniggered. "Them's real good toys," he said. "Real good. One of a kind, you might say."

He took his break before Fred did. Hank was a lot more sure of himself than he had ever been, what with his friendship with Joe.

Fred went about fixing up the place, putting things back where they belonged. Then, something called out—a faraway voice.

Fred turned but he was alone. He didn't think anything of it until it happened a few more times. Had he looked at a toy soldier on the end bottom shelf he'd have seen the thing crying real tears.

# Chapter 29

The clowns were covered in gore. The mutilated remains of one old pissed off carny who had the misfortune of confronting Joe Sabba, along with two detectives investigating his story about murder and mayhem, were ready to be buried.

Happy burped while Noble picked his teeth. Danny hadn't eaten as much as his pals. He was busy guzzling some moonshine, which he had added blood to at Happy's suggestion.

"You were right about the blood. It gives the drink a certain something."

Happy looked proud of himself. "I got the idea from that horror movie you know."

They began discussing Dracula.

"It was nice in them days when Fred used to give us money to go the movies. Sometimes we all went. They thought we were part of the show—must have been our makeup."

"Must have been."

"So what do you think about these guys? What was the beef about? Think it's true, what that guy said?"

"The carny guy? Nah! Bunch of bullshit. All I know," Noble said, "is if Joe is ever in danger, we just have to help! Period."

They all agreed. Protecting Joe was paramount. None of them realized they used to feel that way about Fred.

\*  \*  \*

Joe was the last person Fred expected to see. He was waiting for him near the commissary. "Eat yet?"

Fred hadn't so they went in together. "I'm on my break now. Hank is there."

They ordered coffee and apple pie. Joe insisted on paying for it. That's when he started what Fred always thought of as his charm offensive.

"So Fred, how you doing? How do you like the souvenir shop?"

"It's okay. I'm okay."

Joe gazed intently at him. "I hope you are because I have big plans for this place. That is, Tommy has and we've had a lot of discussions. The receipts are really impressive."

Fred tried to look thrilled but he just found he didn't care. He couldn't explain it—but everything felt more wrong than ever.

Joe jabbered on and didn't appear to notice. Suddenly, he stopped. Fred realized he hadn't paid attention and he felt stupid. "I'm sorry, what was that again?"

Joe laughed. "Too many late nights with Lucy?" He winked. "What I said was, Tommy had this idea about adding certain things to the place. Sure fire stuff. In fact, he thinks this whole place will become a permanent amusement park, along the lines of Coney Island… He wants to speak with you later. I said I'd tell you."

Fred didn't really want to go. He didn't mind Tommy but Mabel was creepy—even creepier than Joe. "Sure, I'll go. What time?" he asked, trying to look earnest.

\*  \*  \*

He showed up at the appointed time. Tommy was as welcoming as anything and Mabel looked thrilled to see him. She dressed a little more conservatively as of late. That is, her sweater wasn't as tight as she usually wore them.

"I'm so glad you could join us," she oozed.

Fred flashed her one of his best practiced smiles.

Joe looked up and waved. They got down to it after talk about the circus and the acts. When they started to talk about Tombo being wanted for rape and murder, Fred almost peed himself.

"Yeah," Joe said. "Can you believe it? He was with a circus owned by this guy I know. Small time stuff. Two women were raped and murdered and Tombo was accused. I was there then and defended the kid right away 'cause I knew it was prejudice, what with Tombo being Spanish. A foreigner, if you please. Granted, he was always a ladies' man but he ain't no killer and he sure doesn't have to rape anyone!"

"How do you know?" Fred asked. He didn't care. It was a fair question.

Joe looked unfazed. "I know because Tombo was with me the night in question. I told the cops that..."

"So he wasn't arrested?"

"Truthfully? We beat it the hell out of there before any further investigation. Do you know Tombo? Hell of a nice guy."

Fred remembered his jealousy upon seeing Lucy flirting with the young man. "Not really..."

Mabel shook her head. "Well, he's safe with us and he'll stay safe."

Fred thought that was one fucking weird remark. Tommy soon changed the subject and drinks were served. It was then that the subject of the funhouse and carousel came up.

"It'll be great. I'd say to have both of them open at the same time but it won't be easy. Still, I'm going to see about hiring some extra workers, and as far as the carousel goes, Mabel and I are going to meet with some people from France in New Orleans next week. They stock the Mardi Gras parades, you see. Into all sorts of stuff like that. We're pretty excited."

Fred didn't know what to think, but tried to look enthused.

"And," Tommy said, "no more huts. If we make this into a real amusement park, there will be regular housing for staff. How does that appeal?"

It did appeal. If only he felt better about the place.

"A house for each of my people, well, couples." Tommy winked. "Maybe if you and Lucy get hitched..."

Mabel giggled. "Wouldn't that be nice," she said.

The others were talking but Fred found himself staring into her eyes. It wasn't that he found her attractive, although she was—it was more a case of finding he couldn't look away. The more he stared, the less he cared.

He joined the conversation then and found to his horror when he turned back to Mabel, she was sitting at the table bare breasted. She didn't even look embarrassed.

Tommy asked Fred if he'd like another drink but before he could answer, Mabel cracked a joke and Fred realized she wasn't naked. He had imagined it.

He kept up as best he could but even as he spoke to them and despite being pleased about the idea of a home, he knew he'd have to see Doc Enright.

# Chapter 30

Doc Enright looked amused. "Bare breasted, eh? Well, maybe wishful thinking?"

Fred was annoyed by his reaction. He was a doctor after all; he'd have preferred he take his admission more seriously. Doc must have realized because he said he probably was tired. "Being overtired can cause such things to happen."

That made Fred feel a bit better. "Look," Doc said. "Just relax. How are you sleeping? Still have those dreams...?"

Fred didn't want to say but he did because Enright was a doctor. "Yeah, sometimes. And I'm still seeing Lucy so I'm not frustrated or anything like that!"

Enright smiled. "I'm glad you are. How do you feel about the Fosters? Any problems?

He was studying him so carefully, Fred began to feel squirmy. "They're okay."

"*But?* Look Fred," Enright said, "you can tell me anything."

"Okay, I find Mrs. Foster a bit weird."

"Why is that?"

"She just is. She seems to flirt too much for a married woman."

When he mentioned the tight sweaters, Enright chuckled. "I think she stimulated that day dream of yours. I guess she is something of a flirt. Folks know that really. And," Enright said, "Tommy seems to look the other way. She's had affairs with a few performers..."

Fred was surprised at Enright telling him such things. Yet, he was pleased. Maybe he said it to help him.

"Some women are like that—some men, too. Just the way they are. Tommy, I think, is just so in love with her he looks the other way."

Doc wanted him to agree. So Fred told him he was probably right.

"Just relax, Fred, and don't worry about everything."

\* \* \*

Joe and Hank stood outside. "Feeling alright?" They annoyed him. They looked uncaring and full of shit, especially Joe.

"I'm fine." Fred expected another question but Joe changed the subject.

"Tommy and Mabel left this morning. You know, to see about the carousel. It'll be great. What do you think?"

Fred smiled but he didn't really know what he thought. Or maybe he did and he was already making plans to get the hell out of there.

\* \* \*

There was a large box of new stock waiting for them. Joe said it had just arrived. "Came early this morning. I had it brought here. What do you think?" Joe asked.

Fred lightly touched their faces. They looked like they were alive or had been. Remarkable. "They look so real…"

"The boy and girl are two of my favorites. They're all very special, one of a kind. That's why they're to be priced more. I thought five bucks each. That's the price from now on."

"But will people pay that much?" Fred was dubious.

"They will, I think. We'll have to see. Hank and I will stock up the place. Why don't you take time off? You look tired."

Fred felt paranoid. He was trying to figure out why Joe told him that, following his words with a smile.

"Go on, go take a load off. Hank and I can do this. I'll see you get paid, don't worry."

How could something that sounded nice sound evil at the same time? Maybe he was cracking up after all.

\* \* \*

Andy had come to watch Old Pa so Fred was able to sleep. When he woke, he gave his father dinner and then turned him back over to Andy. He brought dinner for Andy and himself back from the commissary. After that, he decided to take in the show.

Fred hadn't really seen the acts. He only caught part of them. But that night he wanted to see the whole thing.

The show was something else. Lucy didn't see him sitting there; she was too intent on the stuff she had to do. Somersaulting on a pony isn't easy. It was a great act though and Fred felt proud of her.

Tombo came out next with his dog act. Fred thought about what he had heard, and he wondered. The young man looked handsome dressed as he was in a glittering bolero and tight slacks. He was very theatrical and practiced but it was what the folks wanted. He had the three poodles and a little mutt jumping through hoops.

Each time they did, he blew kisses to the audience. "Don't you love these doggies?" he called.

People shouted back, mostly kids. Fred had to admit he was entertaining and at least as good as the tragic Bob had been.

The clowns milled around, interacting with the audience, kidding and yoking it up with kids and adults. They seemed to be on their best behavior as well.

Fred noticed hot dog vendors walking around. This was something new. The people were going for it though and the stuff wasn't that cheap. Twenty-five cents for a hot dog and fifteen cents for a bag of popcorn. Fred decided Tommy was a dammed good businessman.

The lion tamer was scheduled to precede Queenie, the elephant. He was really good, a real showman. He had two lions and one tiger, and they were work. Snarling and growling and making threatening gestures with their paws. One wrong move and he would have been a goner. Still, he cracked his whip—calling out commands and cajoling them, too.

He didn't turn his back on them though, which Fred thought was a damned good idea. The applause thundered through the space especially when the tiger backed off with its head down, like a pussy cat, all timid and everything.

Next up came Queenie and her handler. Fred liked the young Indian man. He was friendly and kindly to his beloved elephant. She obeyed his commands. And as she was wont to do, she stood on her hind legs on command. The children loved it and everyone gave a massive applause.

Imelda and Ramon looked good, all decked out in their glittering attire. The audience loved them and showed it with their whistling and applauding and gasping. There were moments of high drama when Ramon had to catch Imelda. Fred's heart nearly stopped.

Fred left then. He wanted to check out the Midway to see how his people were doing. If they still were his people. Al and Darla called out to him, looking as happy as ever. He was glad for them but felt sorry for Alice. She was sitting on her throne eating, which pleased the onlookers. They called to her and teased her, but she didn't seem to care.

Fred waved but she didn't notice. He planned to stop by her hut later but in the end, he didn't. Had he done so, he'd have seen what she had there. A few animals lying about—most dead but one or two rodents and rabbits still alive, albeit barely, as they were nearly drained of blood.

How was he to also know Al and Darla would visit her later to join the feast?

# Chapter 31

A lot happened in the time that Mabel and Tommy were away—not that Fred knew about it. He didn't know Alice was a committed vampire, nor did he know that so were Al and Darla. He didn't realize the clowns had begun sniffing out those they wanted to eat, either.

What he did know was, the dolls were really starting to get to him. It always happened when he was alone. He thought he heard things—voices in the distance and crying, sometimes.

He'd look around, even picking up a doll to examine it. He never found the source of it—whatever it was. He wanted to confess to Hank but didn't trust him. Hank and Joe were too close and his secret wouldn't be a secret for long.

There was only one thing to do. He had best see Doc again.

He was about to go into the doctor's office when he heard Joe's voice. He backed away but stayed close enough to listen. Damned if he wasn't in for another shock. The clowns were also there! He first heard Happy's voice. Happy laughed and said they could eat whatever had to be eaten. They were talking about bodies.

When Joe laughed and said, "Those that aren't made into dolls, they could have..."

Fred rushed off then. He thought of going to Lucy, but Al's hut was closer.

The little guy was only too welcoming. He was so nice in fact, Fred just broke down. Al gave him whisky and told him to calm down. "Whatever it is, you can tell me."

Darla looked frightened and Al suggested she give them some privacy. Fred was grateful for that. It would be tough enough just telling him all this crazy shit he had overheard.

He began at once. As he spoke, he tried to gauge Al's reaction because it sounded pretty nuts.

Al looked as though he did believe him. He kept reassuring him. "It does sound crazy though."

Fred agreed. "It fucking does, Al. But it's true. They are killing people...and the dolls...!"

The mention of the dolls set things back, Fred realized. He shouldn't have said anything about them. It sounded too nuts.

"Them dolls, you mean the ones you sell?"

Fred said yes and watched his friend pour himself a drink. When he smiled, Fred began to feel desperate. "It's true. You have to believe me!"

Although Al looked sympathetic, Fred was sure—he didn't believe him.

"You're just tired, Fred. Work and one thing and another. And Old Pa. That's not easy caring for him. You're a good son. I'd have killed my father if I'd been able to...but my father was..."

Al stopped speaking when he caught the look on Fred's face.

"My father's no saint, Al. He's done murder..."

"You told me he had murdered. Look at me and Hank and the clowns..."

Fred let out a loud sob. "It's much worse what he did...you can't imagine."

He was certain Al was going to speak but when he didn't, Fred continued. "My father was wanted... He still is; he always will be...what he did..."

"You can tell me..."

"I've killed, too, Al. I killed to protect him—see, he killed some women..."

*Circus of Horrors*

Fred couldn't get the rest out. Al soothed him, said he could confide in him. "What is it? What's preying upon you, Fred? Something is—Who did your dad kill? You can tell me, honest. I won't tell no one!"

"He killed five prostitutes in Whitechapel in 1888. My dad is Jack the Ripper!"

Al laughed. "Come on, how do you know that? That was before you were born. That's bullshit!"

Fred began to cry. "The box I always kept hidden, the one he liked to look through—those are souvenirs he kept! They're from the women he murdered! There are even body parts! He loves touching them!"

Al just stared at him, the smile gone from his face.

"Two men found us. One was a private dick all the way from England! He showed us papers. The detective said he had given his services for free. He knew the Chief Inspector, Abberline, who was on the case."

"What do you mean?"

"And the other was the grandson of the last victim. Mary Kelly. She had children in Liverpool, they said. Then she went off to London when her man kicked her out.

The family didn't know about her murder, but when they did, they kept pressing the police for information but were always turned away. The son had connections in the press and they got help... See, my father was one of the suspects although he had never been identified as one of the *official* ones."

Al shook his head.

Fred was firm. "No, goddamn it—it's all true! They had papers with them to prove who they were. Photos, too. Pictures of Mary Kelly."

"Are there any?"

Fred leaned forward. "They showed me one. It was awful. I believed everything they said. That is why I killed them!"

Al looked stunned. "You did it to protect your father though..."

Fred collapsed finally, but not before the darkness closed in, after it did.

\*  \*  \*

Darla smiled at him. "Al is over with your father. Andy came for him. He took ill. Don't be scared now. Your dad is alright. You can see him later."

"Later nothing!" Fred said and shot right outside. He saw them just ahead. His father's victims! Their ghosts were back! There were five of them—five female forms reaching out.

They moved in the direction of his hut. Fred saw Al open the door for them. He hollered but it was no good. He could hear Old Pa crying. "Get them off!"

Fred tried but there was nothing to grab; it was like pulling at mist. He started to shout when he saw the souvenirs spread out all over the floor.

Al was laughing—"Are these them?" he asked. Joe and the clowns were present and joined in the laughter, too. Happy was waving something about. "Ain't this an old kidney?" he asked, popping it into his mouth.

The other two clowns called him selfish—that was after Fred had grabbed Old Pa.

"Fuck you! He's my father!"

He turned to see if they were following but they weren't. Old Pa stumbled as they hurried toward the pickup. "Old Pa, please walk, goddamn it!"

The old man was crying. "They hurt me..."

"They won't hurt you anymore! We're getting away!"

*If the fucking truck starts...if no one's done anything to it.*

It started and Fred cried out as he stepped on the gas to get his father the fuck out of there.

He never saw the other ghosts, those he had killed himself, even the ones he'd forgotten about.

# Chapter 32

Dalton was the kind of town that rolled up its sidewalks after five. Fred had no fucking idea where the police department was and there was no one to ask. He just hoped he'd find it. After ten minutes, he spotted the only building with lights on inside. It said Dalton Police.

He burst into the office. The sheriff looked startled. Fred knew he looked crazed—half carrying his father. "I need help!"

That looked like a given. "I'm Sheriff Dean. Is he sick?"

Fred didn't bother to answer. He just sat his father down. "I have to talk to you. I come from..."

"Foster's. I think I saw you there...."

*Yeah, crazy fuckers...*

"I can call a doctor..."

Fred shook his head, laughing. He knew he looked completely crazy now, but he was beyond the point of caring. "Don't call Doc Enright, whatever you do..."

The look on the sheriff's face was priceless. "I know him. He's a fine doctor..."

"Is he?! Is he now?! I don't think so! He's palsy with Joe and Joe is the craziest evil bastard I know!"

Fred was not surprised to see the sheriff lightly touch his gun. He decided he'd better look as normal as possible. "Look, it's like this. The whole place—it's full of evil. There are things going on you would not believe... I know. Believe me! I've seen things... There are dolls. I sell them with Hank. He's one of the midgets. The dolls are weird; they talk sometimes!"

The more he spoke, the nuttier he sounded. Why'd he have to mention the dolls, for Christ sakes?

Dean said he was going to call someone. "I'm phoning my own doctor…"

Fred felt himself begin to relax with that. Now all he had to do was wait.

Old Pa was breathing heavily and looking anxious and he felt uncomfortable waiting there, what with the sheriff staring at him suspiciously and not speaking.

A man came about ten minutes later. "I'm Dr. Lewis. What seems to be the trouble?"

Where could he begin? Everything he would have said sounded nuts. His face was flushed and his eyes looked crazy. The expression on the doctor's face told him that.

The doctor seemed more concerned with Old Pa. "Is he always like that?" Fred nodded. "Sir, can you hear me? Do you know where you are?"

Old Pa was hyperventilating.

"I think we ought to get you both over to the hospital…to check things out."

Check things out! Fred started to laugh—loud maniacal laughter. He couldn't stop. When the doctor and the sheriff looked at one another, he laughed even louder.

"If I'm crazy, I have good reason to be. Anyone in my position would be!"

A lot of things went through his head. He told himself to calm down. He would tell the truth. It would be better if he did. "They know who my dad is. See, that's how it started."

"Your *father*?"

It was so hard for him to get it out. But he did. "My father is Jack the Ripper. You know that famous unsolved case from England?" He watched them carefully as he imparted the secret, that gut-wrenching, fucking secret he had kept all his life.

"Oh sure, Joe guessed it. He went through the souvenirs, see? The Ripper took things... how he found the box the second time beats the hell out of me...!"

"*Jack the Ripper*, you mean?"

Fred nodded. "Yeah, but wait, there's more which involves me... I will tell you..."

He was ready to tell them too, but he found himself being led away.

"Where are you taking me?"

"Sheriff Dean is going to help get you over to the hospital. It's for your own good," the doctor said. "You and your father can stay over there. It isn't far, just to rest for now. Tomorrow you can talk to people."

\* \* \*

It wasn't a long ride. The car stopped and he was helped out. The sheriff kept calming him. Fred wanted to tell him to shut up after a while but he didn't dare.

In they went—a senile old man and his lunatic son. Fred watched his feet moving along the waxed green lino floor. When they stopped, he looked up. A nurse glanced at both of them and asked: "This them?"

*The lunatic father and son.*

She looked serious but then smiled in that frozen way they do sometimes. "We'll see that you get some rest..."

Rest, that was good. "Yes, I need to rest but then I have to tell people..."

"Of course," she said. "That will all be taken care of. Meanwhile, Jim is going to take you to your room."

Jim, the towering orderly, looked like a pro wrestler. He smiled. "I can push you both at the same time."

They were seated, not roughly but firmly, in two wheelchairs.

"I want to thank the sheriff... and..."

"Don't you worry about that. They know you're in good hands."

Fred smiled because the wheelchair felt like a pram. A vague memory of being pushed by his smiling mother came to him and it was comforting.

"Here we are."

The room had two beds. His father had one and he had the other. A nurse came in, a solemn looking one—no fixed smile, just two jowls and a needle. "Just giving you something to relax you."

*Fine by me.*

Pa was soon snoring and Fred began to feel sleepy almost at once. He didn't even wake during the night. He slept straight through, not something he usually did.

\* \* \*

He woke up in his hut without Old Pa. He started to panic but Lucy was sitting beside the bed. "It's okay. He's enjoying himself. You will, too. Nothing to worry about. They brought you both back. Everything will be fine, Fred. Just relax."

"Who brought us back? And when did they take Old Pa? He's not with Joe, is he?"

She wouldn't answer. She kept telling him to calm down and he couldn't fucking stand it anymore. "Let me calm you down, Fred," she said as she slipped in beside him. He recoiled and she shook her head. "I can make you happy. It doesn't have to be like this."

She leaned over to kiss him but he froze. She put his hand on her breast. "I can get naked for you, Fred. How about it?"

He pushed her so hard, she fell onto the floor. Then he apologized and helped her up when he heard what sounded like carousel music.

"That's the merry go round, Fred. Isn't it great? It's all set up. Fast, huh?"

Yeah fast, but he didn't really give a shit.

"I love that kind of music. Don't you?" Lucy asked as she unzipped his pants.

"Fuck you!" he cried, pushing her away.

"Now Fred, language!"

"Go to hell. I have to see my father!" He flung the door open but he couldn't move. In front of him revolved carousel horses with children on them. Painted horses galloping around the place; carousel horses that *weren't* on the carousel!

"They come and go like that. The kids love it," Lucy said. "It's like magic for them."

But it wasn't like magic. They didn't love it at all because they were shouting for their parents to save them. The only ones that didn't shout were those that fell under the hoofs. And the reason they couldn't shout was because the horses were killing them.

# Chapter 33

He had never seen an apocalypse, nor was he conversant with the one depicted in the Bible in Revelations. Had he been, he might have known what could happen.

What he saw was bedlam. The horses were running wild with children hanging onto them, and no one was trying to stop them, not even the workmen. They stood there, watching. Only Andy made a brave attempt to help, but he was soon felled and stomped to death.

He shouted, "I die in Christ!"

Fred didn't have time to think about what he meant. He would, of course, remember it later.

People shouted instructions to those who tried to stop the horses but there were no bridles to grab because these were not living horses.

The cries of the children were pitiful. And it seemed with each shout, the horses only galloped more quickly. Despite the children trying to hang on to them, they were soon thrown off one by one.

Before any could scramble away, the monstrous horses doubled back to stomp on them. Fred was certain he heard bones breaking. Bystanders were crying out and those who Fred assumed were parents had flung themselves forward to try and protect their children.

It proved impossible—so many were crushed under the heels of these strange beings. So many children had been stomped to death, although one or two were still alive—screaming. Their parents were screaming too, trying to comfort them and calling for help, pleading for it, shouting for it. Fred ran to help, but it was overwhelming. "We need help here!" he shouted. "Please!"

The clowns came over but not to help. They had gathered like vultures. Kneeling down, they seemed to gloat. A man—one of the parents no doubt—grabbed Happy's collar and shouted at him. Another began punching and swearing at him.

The other clowns came to his defense. Noble and Danny were more than a match for any would be attacker as their nails were long and could easily shred flesh. The man was killed instantly. When your throat's torn out, death is imminent.

When the clowns saw Fred staring at them, they shouted almost in unison: "We're getting it done. It is the appointed time! Don't you understand anything?"

The clowns had killed everyone off—all the parents and the surviving children and anyone else that hadn't been stomped and kicked to death. "Dig in, boys!" Happy shouted. As soon as he spoke the order, they began to feed, shoving handfuls of bloody flesh in their mouths.

The Wildman of Zanzibar was ecstatic. "It's like a miracle!"

Fred shouted himself hoarse. He condemned and begged, cursed and pleaded. Happy threw over a chunk of bloodied flesh. "Try it, you'll like it," he said.

Fred couldn't even reply but he felt hands on him and heard a voice telling him to stand up. *Joe.* Fred took a swing at him, but Joe only laughed. "You can't hurt me. Don't you know that yet?"

Fred spat at him. Someone laughed loud, raucous laughs. Baby Alice, wearing her favorite pink dress, was sitting on two men. One kicked about but the other lay still. Fred felt certain he was dead. Alice's chin and chest were drenched with blood. "Like wine!" she said. "Just like wine. And me! I never even liked the stuff!"

Fred watched her bend. Joe pointed. "She's sucking on the guy's throat. He'll be dead soon. She's a natural, don't you think? I always knew she was…"

Fred tried to put his hands over his ears, but his arms didn't move. Joe's magic. Joe was grinning. "Come on, Fred, your father is waiting for you in the funhouse! Yes, it's all there for you to see. Everyone likes a funhouse."

He wouldn't go. He tried to make his legs stiff, but Joe was so strong. "You can't fight me. Don't you know that? Come along. Be a good boy!"

As hard as he tried, it was no good. He was pulled along—stumbling and pleading, but pulled along anyway. Joe stopped. "Listen. Ever hear anything like that before?"

The singing came from some place close by. Fred didn't want to listen but he found he had to. He couldn't resist that sound, and the song was the most beautiful he had ever heard. Great birds circled overhead—the largest he had ever seen.

"Ever see anything like that?!"

But they weren't birds!

Fred cried out when he recognized Dorinda. She was screeching and laughing—swooping down on people, picking them up only to toss them aside. And she wasn't alone; there were other winged creatures like her!

"The others are the dancing girls. You'd never know it, would you?! And remember the dreams you had? Hell! Well, you'll see." Joe winked.

Suddenly, Fred felt himself lifted up. Dorinda had snatched him in her claws for she no longer had hands.

The massive claws punctured his flesh, but the pain soon eased because he felt himself slipping into unconsciousness. He didn't though. Dorinda wouldn't let him. She started to sing and he had to listen.

The thing was, while he did, he saw the carnage all around, below him—the grass was saturated with blood and stained with gore.

It was then that he noticed a large building. It was painted red and had a big demon on the front.

"Ain't that good?" Dorinda asked. "That's the new funhouse."

That was where he was dropped. He landed on his face, bleeding, but he didn't care. He only got up to see the monstrous winged beast of a siren fly away.

It was indeed the new funhouse. Old Pa stood behind Al and Darla. Al brought him forward. "Your dad is good with a knife. Darla and me, we never seen anything like it."

Fred shook his head. "What are you talking about—" He stopped when he saw his father covered in blood. Al took the knife from him. "Actually, it's a straight razor," he said. "You should see the people he carved up. Come, Joe will show you. You'll love it!"

# Chapter 34

Old Pa was covered in blood.

"He worked up a frenzy but then kind of stopped. Still, he's with you now so that's good."

Fred steadied his father when he nearly toppled over. Joe reached out to help. "We don't need your help!"

"Okay, Fred. Have it your way. Only this is what it's all about. This is my bit now. It's what I have to do," Joe said.

"What the hell are you talking about?"

Joe sighed. "You're all the same. Every single fucking one of the damned is the same. You just don't get it."

"My father—!"

"Was fucking Jack the Ripper! Yes! That's a start!"

Fred felt his knees nearly give way. "Start?"

Joe knew everything…

"You killed more people than you think you did. That's for starters. That's what this is leading to, but hey! Don't flatter yourself. It isn't all about you or your dad. It's about a whole lot more!"

Fred backed up, which only made Joe laugh. "Oh, yes, it is! It's all part of a much bigger picture. A grand design, if you will!"

Fred turned to run but some unseen force pulled him back. Joe's voice was almost gentle. "It's too late to leave. " He gestured toward the funhouse. "It's waiting for you in there. You'll see. Come on. Everyone loves a funhouse!"

With that, the doors opened. Big fucking massive metal doors banging open. As soon as they did, scores of bodies fell out, all bloodied and mutilated.

Joe gestured toward them. "Nosey parkers, jerkoffs, would-be heroes... thought they could save their town." Joe shook his head. "Saps... It's like Al said, your dad is good with a knife."

Joe raised his arms and said something—whatever it was, it sounded like an incantation. It was then that Old Pa began to speak, not in his usual gibberish but in complete sentences. "I don't want to be here," he said. "Get me out, Son." He started to sob. Fred tried soothing him but it was no good. He sobbed even louder—gut-wrenching, shattering sobs. Joe shook his head. "Too late for any remorse now, you old fucker. No sir, the time's come—it's judgment day." He motioned toward a gondola. "That's for you and sonny boy, see? It's just like them ones in Venice. You'll feel like you're sailing."

They didn't see Hank sitting in the back at first, not until he waved.

"Hank will conduct the tour, boys. He knows how. He's a quick learner." Hank looked visibly moved by his mentor's words. "It'll be the ride of your lives!"

They got in. There was no choice. They were sitting in the damned thing before they knew it.

"Ain't it great?" Hank said. "Just relax. You ain't seen nothing yet!"

\* \* \*

Hank talked a mile a minute. Laughed a lot, too—brimming with happiness. He told Fred and Old Pa things they had never known. All about himself and how devoted he was to Joe. "He is my teacher and my lover. Our love will last throughout eternity. He leaned over and in a confidential tone of voice added: "I promised to serve him as the others did. He has my soul."

That last tidbit barely registered.

Before Fred could even think of replying, another door banged open. Hank rubbed his hands. "This is it, fellas. Just sit back and watch!"

Watch they did as all sorts of things happened. Crazy looking stuff shot out at them, just as in all funhouses or rides of this kind. Only this was different. The place smelled funny. Fred noticed it first. "That smells like a city…"

It was the familiar stink of vomit and shit.

"Like a dirty, overcrowded section of a city, maybe? Recognize it? It's just like being back, ain't it?"

Old Pa cried out because he saw the city that he knew so well. "I know that place!"

"That's right," Hank said. "Recognize that as your old stomping grounds?"

It was like watching a film. A man walked down the slime-covered cobblestones. A prostitute called out to him. "Care for a little fun? I'll let you fuck me good and proper, I will."

The man turned briefly but even in profile, Fred saw that it was his father. He knew the truth, but seeing it like this was something else!

He watched as this younger representation of his father shook his head. He was repulsed by the woman. That was obvious. Still, he followed her.

"She's heading for Buck's Row!" Old Pa cried out. "Oh, Christ!"

And so she was. When she lifted up her skirts and dropped her knickers, Fred's father strangled her. She tried to break away but there was no chance. She couldn't even cry out.

"Fuck me, will you, you slut."

Hank leaned over. "Joe showed me this many times. It's really interesting. He has these powers, you see."

The slashing lasted quite some time. Old Pa couldn't get over it. "I never remembered it lasting that long!"

"Well it did, old man. You were in a frenzy, really loving it. Now for the disembowelment," Hank announced. "He really was a master, like an artist."

The so-called master worked feverishly.

"Took a piece of broken mirror and then you ran, didn't you? You vanished in the alleys."

*Circus of Horrors*

Old Pa nodded. "There were so many alleys and warrens..."

Fred knew that. Whitechapel had been like that for centuries.

Hank again: "That is of course why they never caught you. Though it wasn't for lack of trying. Queen Victoria kept deluging them with letters asking why the murderer hadn't been caught!"

Old Pa was crying but it wasn't over. "No," Hank said. "There's more. This next one for instance!"

The scene changed. "It's Hanbury Street! I remember!"

"See," Hank said. "All that confusion for all those years. Seeing your dark deeds is clearing that all up. How's it look, old man?"

"She seemed nice. I remember that smile." He sobbed.

Hank nodded. "Annie Chapman had been respectable; well, more than the others. That's true. Joe told me that. But there she is, lifting her skirts. Waiting for you to stick it in."

"She said I could fuck her for a shilling. But I didn't have a shilling. I had been robbed. I might have..."

"No," Hank said. "You'd have killed her anyway. You liked it. Joe told me. You really went to town on this one. Those bits you took from her guts are all dried out now and in your little souvenir box! The ones you like to play with, aren't they? From the fucking box Fred buried!" Fred turned to hit Hank, who only laughed because an unseen force punched Fred hard in the face. "They're with me on my side, not yours, stupid. Watch."

They watched and watched until Fred began to vomit. His father didn't; he just kept crying. "'I was sick then—insane...!"

"You were evil. Evil knows evil, old man. Now you've come home. But really!"

When Old Pa wept on Fred's shoulder, Hank made him turn around. "If you don't, they'll turn your head for you." Old Pa obeyed. Hank laughed. "Good, now look! See? What's this—two in one night, ain't it? Mitre Square. Why'd you do up her face the way you did? Catherine Eddowes."

"I was mad. I should have been put away."

"But you weren't, not ever. You liked it. You only think you didn't look!'

They all looked and it was true. The monster that was Old Pa as a young man looked to be enjoying himself.

"Tell the truth, man—you thought of fucking her when her guts were hanging out, didn't you?"

Vociferous denials ensued.

"Watch."

Fred saw the Ripper fondle the woman's mutilated breasts. And then, he heard him sigh.

"Course you weren't through. There was another one. You saw her and she led you down another street. She was chewing cashews. She gave you one. Remember?"

Old Pa tried to get out of the gondola but Fred stopped him.

"Then you saw someone—see? That man there. And you panicked before you could cut her up!"

Old Pa had collapsed on Fred's shoulder. Hank left them alone only for a few moments. "Come on, now. Time to face facts!"

Fred pleaded for his father.

Hank shook his head. "The show must go on! The best is last. Miller Court, the pretty young one. Remember?"

Old Pa did. And though he tried to protest, to entreat some pity, it was no good. Hank, like one of Hell's best demons, went on: "You wanted to fuck her brains out but you couldn't get it up. You only got it up with Fred's mother and that was only a few times. See, Joe knows all of this!"

Fred saw his younger father looking at his limp penis. The young prostitute told him not to feel badly. "I could have used the money, like," she said, "rent's overdue. But you come back some time and I'll give you a time you won't ever forget."

Hank gave a brittle laugh. "You gave it to her then though, didn't you?"

The three of them watched as the girl was literally eviscerated.

"Why'd you pile that stuff up the way you did? All that skin and organs?"

No answer, just more crying and begging to be let out.

"Show ain't over yet, fellas. Not by a long shot," Hank said. "There's a lot of ground to cover. This is about you, Fred!"

# Chapter 35

Fred started to argue with Hank. That was when it happened. A terrible stench assailed him. Old Pa was gagging and then, so did Fred. Hank laughed.

Fred started to tremble and when another pair of doors banged open, he closed his eyes, trying to steel himself against what was coming. Hank demanded he look and he did.

There was a room he recognized at once, with its familiar pale green wallpaper with big pink roses.

"The house in Queens."

Old Pa nodded. "It was nice. If you hadn't..."

Hank laughed. "Queens, New York. You liked it. Too bad you did what you did. Go on. What did you do you, Fred?"

He didn't answer, but then again, he didn't have to. It was all played out for him. He saw a young man answer the door.

"Look at you!" Hank laughed. "What were you, about twenty-five there?"

Fred didn't answer but Hank just went on. "That's the parlor. Right? It was good you were fixing a loose floorboard. Your hammer came in handy..."

Fred didn't reply. He was too fixated on what he was seeing. He watched his younger self open the door. Two men stood there, one in a three piece suit and the other dressed more casually.

The three piece suit spoke first. "Does Mr. Charles Dodger live here?"

"Who wants to know?" the young Fred asked.

Three piece suit said one sentence. Just the one. And Fred let him in. "I know who your father is."

The other man who looked like a laborer didn't speak at all. Not at first. It was the suit that did all the talking. "My name is Celadean and I was hired to investigate the Ripper killings... This is Mr. James Kelly, the grandson of Mary Kelly...the Ripper's last victim..."

The young Fred spoke calmly. "Why come here?"

Celadean told him. He gave dates, names, and facts. "This is an open and shut case. I will be wiring Scotland Yard later today."

The young Fred laughed nervously. "This is ridiculous. My father and I have been in the United States for many years... He was nowhere near London when those killings occurred. Don't you check anything?

The suit shook his head and rattled off a litany of all the facts he said he had checked. "I have proof your father resided in Whitechapel..."

It got violent when Fred told them to leave. When he threatened to phone the police, the suit laughed. But the grandson whipped out a razor. "Same for same," he said. The suit shook his head. "No, James, I'll have none of that."

Fred had, by this time, grabbed the hammer. He moved so quickly, they hardly had time to react. They were alive one second and dead the next, with their skulls caved in.

Hank winced. "Christ! I could hear the bones shattering!"

Fred tried to console his father.

"And that's when you went nuts, old man. That one incident did it. Your own fair-haired boy did these two."

Old Pa started with the gibberish again.

"Old man, you forgot about it because you wanted to. But you remember it really. Funny thing, the mind. It can be so selective."

Now the scene changed again as the gondola drifted past two more open doors.

"You took them in your truck and dumped them in Secaucus in the marshes. Favorite dump for bodies. You wrapped them up good though so none of their brains or blood left a trail. Then you fucked off to California. You changed your names, too."

They had; everything Hank said was true. There was no reason to deny anything.

"But there's more. Something that might have slipped your mind in the intervening years, Fred…"

They saw a house. Fred let out a muffled cry because he suddenly remembered it.

"The boarding house in San Jose. Mrs. Montrose ran it. Remember her? She was nice to both of you. Her husband had a stroke, dragged his leg around. Tragic really, but that wasn't the most tragic thing…"

Fred began to retch. He pleaded with Hank not to go on.

"Oh, but Fred, I have to go on. That's the purpose of this whole thing! There was a daughter. Not right in the old cabesa. Her name was Mildred…"

Fred shouted for Hank to stop. "Please, I beg you. Please."

Hank didn't even answer. "Sure, she must have weighed about two hundred pounds. She was kindly, nuts, but always smiled. You liked her. She was always giving you something, little presents. Crappy stupid stuff like broken pencils and half eaten apples. But she did it in such a way as to be nice. You were always polite to her, too. But then something happened."

Fred shook his head. "No, nothing that I can recall…we moved out…"

"Sure, you moved out *after* that. Sure did. You went across the country. You both fucked off because you were scared."

Fred protested, but Hank waved him off and continued. "Golly, Fred. Don't you remember what you did? Maybe this will refresh your memory."

They saw Mildred sitting in his room. She had found the metal box. "You know what box that is, don't you, kid? That metal strong box?"

*Circus of Horrors*

Fred started to speak but stopped because his younger self came into the room. He started shouting at the fat woman and she tried to get up fast but she was too fat.

"How dare you! Those are personal things. You have no right...!"

The more he spoke, the more upset she became. He began to strangle her when she started to scream. Her face grew purple and her tongue protruded. His face was a vision of madness and also one of exhilaration because he was expunging his enemy once and for all.

She went limp and it was only then that he looked to be sensible. His face had turned red and he was sweating. He ran out of the room but not before taking the strong box.

"You and your father left that night. The police knew you did it. They searched for you both but got nowhere because you beat it the hell out of there and you changed your names again. You called yourself the names you use now. Fred and Charlie Dodger. Hot stuff, like the artful dodgers you are. Let me show you what happened though."

The scene changed and Fred saw the landlady hanging because she had killed herself after the murder.

"Yeah, sad, don't you think? And the husband and father didn't last long. The second stroke proved fatal. How do you feel now?"

Fred laughed mirthlessly. "How do you think I feel?"

"Like shit?"

That he didn't answer; he only tried not to cry while he comforted his father.

Hank leaned forward. "Would it help you if I said I felt sorry for you? Well, I do. Honest. See, it's not me. I'm more like the good cop. It's Joe—Joe serves at a higher level than me—I'm just a raw recruit." It seemed that Hank waited for a response but there wasn't any. "Oops, it's starting again. Let's see what happens."

Neither father nor son looked up. They were too upset.

"I get to show it to you. Joe wants me to and I'm honored. Now, it's show time. You saw the past. Kind of like that old classic Christmas Carol story. Well, here's the present—in fact, you'll be seeing the present *and* the future.

Fred tried pleading but it didn't work. Hank just laughed at him. Fred was still crying when two other doors banged open.

"This is what it's all about," Hank said. "Might as well watch it."

Who would have guessed there were so many ghosts floating behind—a load of them now.

# Chapter 36

Fred was screaming when the damned thing started moving again. He had lost all sense of reason, and the fact Old Pa was wailing didn't bother him at all.

This whole thing was a nightmare and a half. Hank had this spiel going about what was coming next but Fred couldn't get it. "Now, this is important. From here on in, the ride gets serious. It may frighten you but there ain't nothing you can do about it." Hank paused for a moment. "Now this next bit—the self-deception ends here. Joe knows you really forgot about this stuff. Do you recall any of the other murders you committed?"

Fred was furious. "I didn't murder anyone else, you fucking bastard! What I did was bad enough, but I only tried to protect my dad!'

Hank shook his head. "Not always. Time to face the truth, *your* truth, my friend.

*His* truth?

"This is it, kiddo. Your truth now. All of it! Watch!"

Fred saw a movie theater he didn't recognize. Not until the movie started, a silent with Greta Garbo. He thought he remembered seeing it.

"See that woman sitting by herself?"

He saw a woman watching the film. He could see her face; it looked pretty in the flickering light. Someone leaned over her holding something. At first he couldn't tell what it was but then, the light from the screen shone on the blade.

A fast movement followed and the woman slumped backwards, her throat cut.

"It's like another mouth, isn't it?"

Fred was leaning forward now. Who was that? It wasn't him. "Why are you showing me this?"

Hank sighed. "I'm showing you because *you're* the one that killed her."

Finally, Fred realized it *was* him, a younger version of himself. He gasped when he saw his younger self take the woman's scarf, but not before dabbing her neck.

"You were in a hurry to get out of there, but you wanted a souvenir."

Fred returned to sobbing when the gondola began to move again.

"Now, don't think that it ended there. It didn't; you liked it. Watch."

The scene changed and Fred saw himself handling those souvenirs of his father's. He'd smell them and rub them on his naked body. Then laugh.

"See, it excited you. It got you hard and that's when you killed."

Now there was scene after scene of women he raped and murdered.

"You killed five more. So you beat your father. You really did, imagine that! The woman in the movies and these."

There followed another woman, middle aged with spectacles. She was holding some books.

"She was a teacher, Fred. And you killed her. See her walking down the dark street? That's you there."

Fred watched as the woman was dragged into an alley and strangled.

"Now this is weird," Hank said.

Fred let out a sob when he watched himself rape the woman.

"She was *dead*! Dead and you did that! Do you know how sick that made you? You were only in your twenties."

He couldn't say anything. He watched the rest of the scenes, those visualizations of what he had done, in silence.

"The woman at the door, a housewife and mother with two kids in school—you asked her if you could use the telephone. When she let you in, you strangled her also. You took a lock of hair from her. And from the next two."

Fred watched, and wept. Yes, there were two more. They were middle aged. "No more raping now—but you did fondle them after you killed them. See?"

"Please..."

"Please what?"

"You took earrings and rings. Just keepsakes. You kept them in a shoe box under your bed."

Fred clapped both hands on his mouth. There it was! The shoe box! Hank smiled. "Here it is. See?"

The image showed him with the open box on his lap! He touched a few things. "I remember...I—"

"Of course you do. It was ages ago but the memory comes back! All the denying shit is out of the way!"

Fred tried to get out of the gondola but Hank stopped him. That is, an unseen force did. "Come on, it's no use! You have to watch! You might as well know."

Something screeched; it sounded like a crow. Dorinda again, flying all over the place. Soaring and dipping and cackling as she did. She was soon joined by three other flying demons.

"Dorinda and her sirens are real demons! Look! Now this is the fun part," Hank said. "Being a demon, they have no gender. It's the most amazing thing!"

Sure enough, Dorinda turned into other things, as did her sirens. They all kept changing into demons with hard-ons, massive and erect, like tree limbs!

Hank was giggling. "Talk about being hung. Fantastic, isn't it?"

Fred surprised Hank when he said, "Go fuck yourself."

Hank laughed. "I don't have to. That's the great part about it—we all get fucked one way or the other. Look, Fred!"

Fred saw some of the demons were heading for the gondola. They pulled him and Old Pa out. Fred tried to fight them and Old Pa did too in his feeble way.

But it was no good. Their pants were pulled down and they were both sodomized. No amount of pleading helped. The demons laughed at them, grunted and howled their pleasure. Then, they changed suddenly into the workmen from the circus. And if that wasn't crazy, there were some people he recognized from the commissary, the cook and some of the other help.

The cook turned into a lizard and then a snake. But it was only when he had returned to his human form that he and the female staff began to copulate.

Fred thought he was going to faint. But Hank told him no one faints in Hell. "And if you did faint, you'd miss something, and it's all too good to miss! Look! There's the mayor and his wife and friends! See?"

He did see. They lay naked and fucking one another. And if that didn't shock, the sheriff and his doctor were joining in.

"It's amazing," Hank said. "They can go on like that forever!"

It didn't seem possible but there was worse than this because Joe suddenly appeared. Fred shouted when he saw him. "Easy, boy. Just more of the tour. You can't see them. Hell, Hank can't see them. But there are a truckload of ghosts following you!" Joe waved his arms. "Now, you both can see them!"

Fred did. There were five of them. The five his father had killed all those years ago. Five women, most of them badly cut up—the fifth was the most horrifying for she was the ghost of Mary Kelly, the most mutilated of the five. All of them converged on Old Pa, screeching as they did.

"Help me! Fred!" he cried but Fred could do nothing because just as he tried to help, his own ghosts appeared. All those he had killed.

The murdered detective and the relative of Mary Kelly looked much as they did in life and death, especially with the backs of their heads caved in. They reached out toward him and began to pummel him, tearing handfuls of hair out. And if that was bad, the fat woman with the wild eyes and protruding tongue was worse. There was no mistaking her girth or the bulging eyes. It was Mildred, the woman he had strangled. "I was only looking!" she said. Then she began wailing.

Someone tried to calm her—her mother, with the rope still around her neck. "You killed my daughter, you monster!"

Behind her was a man Fred knew as the father. "Didn't we suffer enough? You bastard!" He lunged at Fred, digging his fingernails into his flesh. Behind them stood the other five women he had killed. Murdered cruelly and then forgotten! Now they came toward him, bloodied and defiled, tearing and biting him.

Fred cried out for the pain was fierce. Hank laughed. "They're ghosts but they can inflict pain. Surprising, isn't it? Only people who are damned know that. It's a pretty good secret for most of the world though—folks only know it shortly before purgatory!"

Suddenly, Doc Enright and Don appeared with Lucy, Lester, Tombo, and the Wildman of Zanzibar. Along with Dexter, they were all naked, each going down on the other and switching to take turns. The Gorilla Lady too opened her legs wide and was mounted at once, after which two demons had her—one from the front and one from the back.

Lester held up his arms. "You never knew!"

"No, too stupid!" Joe said. "Fred, all those tattoos, they aren't just bullshit, they're incantations—they're for summoning demons!"

Fred could only stare. Joe laughed. "Some orgy, right? Don't look so shocked; they're all servants of Satan. They've been demonized. They're immortal now. Look at the clowns!"

The clowns were screwing one another and whoever else they could get hold of. They consorted with the demons, all of them changing places, too. Lucy asked Fred to take her but he couldn't move. She laughed at him and was instead mobbed by a stream of demons. The sounds they made revolted him.

"Oh, it gets better," Hank said. You'll see. I can't wait for you to see what's next."

Imelda and Ramon appeared waving as they did in their high wire act, only this time they were naked. Demons fondled them. Imelda was taken by three of them at the same time. Ramon was carried off by larger, winged demons. How he laughed. "If I had known Hell was going to be like this, I'd have begged to be let in!"

The entire fucking circus appeared next, but nothing looked real, not the elephant or big cats. Even the ponies Lucy rode and the dogs Tombo worked with looked odd—one dimensional.

"The circus was just sorcery," Hank said then. "Joe's conjuring tricks. You thought it was real!"

The carousel horses followed, bloodied and stained from stomping so many people to death. Bedlam all over again—a lunatic nightmare. Fred took Old Pa in his arms to calm him. How do you calm someone in Hell?

"I know what you're thinking," Joe said. "This is Hell. Well, you'll know the truth of that before too long."

Lucy flew over to Fred once again. "Come on! I know what you like! I can go down on you! I'll make the bells ring for you!" She opened her mouth and Fred gazed into what looked like flames. "Go on," she said. "I won't burn your dick. You'll like it. I promise!"

Fred tried to push her away, but each time he reached out, she moved somewhere else.

"You can't touch demons. They can touch you but you can't touch them! Don't you know anything?" Hank asked.

Fred tried to answer. He tried so hard to formulate a sentence but he couldn't, and when Old Pa was carried off by demons, he could only watch. He couldn't even scream any more.

Hank pointed. "They're going to do to him what he did to his victims!"

## Chapter 37

He didn't have to wait long. The ghosts started attacking Old Pa at once. Unlike before when they pummeled him, they were now slashing him. They didn't appear to be holding a weapon. After all, how can insubstantial beings hold a knife? This was a different sort of assault.

They soon had him on his back just as he had done to them. They tore at his clothes as they slashed away, each taking turns and shrieking as they did.

"Anger never dies," Joe said. And he kept repeating it.

Fred could do nothing but watch. Even when he closed his eyes at the most horrific of times, he felt an unseen force raising his eye lids, forcing him to watch.

Joe laughed. "You have to watch. It's just the way it is."

So he did. When his father had been reduced to a slashed up bloody mass of flesh, courtesy of the ghosts, Fred was hysterical. "No," Joe said. "He isn't dying, just as he's no longer really living. And you're not really living, either, so don't sweat it."

Fred looked shocked, which made Joe laugh. "You can't be that stupid. I mean, I didn't figure you for a genius, but really! You have to know where you are, Son!"

With that, Old Pa was delivered over by demons, and put beside Fred. He was in agony, with his throat cut so deeply, Fred could see through to his spinal cord. Despite that, he was able to speak!

"Get me away! Fred, get me out of here!"

Joe shook his head. "You can't get away now. It's much too late for that... The ghosts are here."

"Damned right they are!" Joe laughed at his own joke.

"But they're in Hell *with* us?"

"It's an agreement between us and the Light World. Those who suffer are given the choice of revenge. If they choose revenge over forgiveness, they come here and get to do what they like." When Fred wept, Joe shook his head. "It has its compensations. They don't burn with the rest of the lot. They just have to stay here and smell the brimstone. But shit, boy. Getting to do what you want has rewards of its own!"

"I can't stand it anymore!"

"Oh, but you have to! You ain't got a choice."

Fred was about to say something, but the gondola started to move forward.

"You're in for a treat here, fellas!"

Sure enough, after the doors banged open, Mabel appeared. She was soon sitting next to Fred, groping him and grinning as she did. When she leaned over to kiss him, she forced his mouth open with her tongue. But it wasn't her tongue that was going into his mouth; it was a slithering serpent! He started to gag because the damned thing kept going in, farther and farther.

Mabel laughed. Soon, other things were coming out of her mouth, this time not snakes but lizards. And toads, small and large ones, toppled onto the floor and began climbing all over him and his father.

Mabel got to cavorting with Joe, each of them in hysterics.

"Ain't too bright, either one of them," Joe said, and Mabel agreed.

Fred watched Joe take Mabel from behind but suddenly, they both turned into other beings, first Mabel then Joe. Now, they'd become winged demons. And if that wasn't crazy enough, Tommy appeared as himself but he soon changed, too. A voice asked, "How do you like it, Fred?" It was Mabel; only she wasn't Mabel or even a regular demon. She was another sort of being entirely.

Fred looked up to see this towering creature, a massive winged being that began to step forward, all covered in scales and open sores. A strange light glowed in its eyes, a light which, when directed at something, could burn that thing. The being stood still for a moment before it once again changed into a handsome young man.

Now it looked like a winged Greek God from antiquity, muscular, beautiful with handsome features—the eyes his greatest asset, large and luminous. Fred found he could not look away.

"Once I was the favored angel. Lucifer the Morning Star, a prince among the angels ..."

Joe hurried over and sank to his knees. "Adored one!" he cried as he took Lucifer's massive organ into his mouth. Fred retched but Lucifer only laughed and before long, turned into the monstrous king of all demons, known as His Satanic Majesty.

His laughter, Joe's and Hank's carried to them, deafening. Fred and Old Pa screamed as the rest of the demons and those that chose to give away their souls joined in the laughter. All of them—Lucy, Doc Enright, Dexter, Don, Lester, Tombo, Imelda and Ramon. It was Joe who said it. "This is a gateway to Hell, boys! Didn't you guess that?!"

Fred had actually known. Old Pa didn't.

"It is to be your eternity. It has been this way ever since the beginning of all beginnings," Satan added. "There are such gateways all over!"

When Fred began to plead, Satan said to get ready. "Both of you better be prepared for you have yet to arrive in Hell. This is only the first taste, more like a vestibule."

Loud, discordant laughter continued all around them. It rang in Fred's ears. He held his hands over his father's ears and pleaded for mercy.

That only made the demons, along with His Satanic Majesty, laugh harder, and as for Joe, he merely repeated what was said before: "Hell is Hell."

Fred looked up when he felt the first blast of heat. It seemed to come from all around him, glowing like burning coal. There was so much of it, spanning one side of the place to the other. Every so often, great bursts of flame shot out from all sides.

"It gets better, but you'll have to wait," Joe said.

# Chapter 38

The heat was intense, no doubt about it. Things began catching fire; bits of wood and wallpaper started burning and those scary popup things every funhouse has were all beginning to burn, too.

"We're burning!" Fred hollered, but Joe only waved him off.

"You only feel like you're burning but you're really not! Feel your skin."

He felt his and his father's too, and Joe was right. Neither of them felt hot, only warm—not even very warm.

"Amazing, isn't it?"

The gondola began to move again. "Wait till you see this! Now this is really something!" Joe said.

At first, Fred didn't see anything. At first. But then he spotted a beautiful looking woman, tall and slim, dressed in a figure hugging gown. She smiled and turned, holding her arms out as fashion models do. Fred was incredulous.

"That's Alice!" Fred shook his head. Joe laughed. "Oh, that's her alright. She looks different now, but that's because she has to."

Alice looked up, still smiling. She was gorgeous. Fred studied her features and saw it was really her.

She kept touching herself, smoothing her hands down her narrow waist and hips. "If this is Hell, Fred, I want more!" Her smile widened. "Ain't I lovely?"

Gone were the great folds of fat, the doughy, dimpled mounds of flesh that made up the being known as Baby Alice. Joe hurried to her. "Let's show him what she's got."

He pulled Alice's gown off so that she was completely naked. Her breasts were now perfect. Joe licked one pert mound. "Don't you love how they turn up? And look here, at her snatch. There it is, no longer covered up by fat!"

Joe invited Fred to try her out, but he didn't move.

"Okay, can't force you—well, I could but I won't. There's more to show you. Now you're going to see the future, and why Alice needs to be the way she is. She's one of the chosen! His Majesty's chosen! Yup, Satan fucked her and liked it." Joe shrugged. "He's like that. She's special to him now."

Fred didn't want to hear any more but Joe said he had to. Now began portents of the future, incidents displayed showing Alice in action.

"She'll be doing Satan's bidding and mine, too. She'll be seducing married men; men who will commit suicide or kill their girlfriends; men who will kill their wives and children for the love of her. She will drive them nuts with her charms."

Fred kept shaking his head.

Alice held up her hand. "This ring is the start. I want diamonds all over the place. Joe said he'd hang them from my nipples if I wanted. I think that would look nice, don't you?"

Fred backed away but Joe was waiting for him. "She's just excited, poor kid. Really though, Fred. This is the future. These things will happen. No doubt about it. See, after they are used, she can do as she likes. Watch."

Fred saw Alice feeding on men she was servicing. Suddenly, sex turned into voracious feeding as he heard sounds of sucking and slurping once again, only now there was blood…torrents of it. Alice laughed. Her chin dripped blood and her teeth were awash with it. The men began to convulse even as she fed more.

"She likes blood more than she ever liked food, Fred, honest!"

And so she did.

"She can drain a man in minutes. I've never seen anything like it," Joe claimed.

Alice began to head for Fred, which made Joe laugh. "She wants you now. She'll get you off just fine if you don't mind her gnawing your dick."

Fred screeched and Joe laughed. Some seconds passed. When Fred next looked up, he saw Al and Darla. Joe hugged them both. "You have been a lot of fun, both of you. And because you please me, I have a surprise for you. I am going to transform you both into something quite magical."

Darla started to clap. "Like Alice? Oh, I want to be beautiful! I long to be! Al looked suspicious and when Darla noticed, she looked frightened.

Joe laughed. "It's not what you think, cutie pies."

As Joe waved his arms, they both cried. It happened in an instant. They were no longer flesh and blood, but dolls. Joe tapped them on their chests. "See? They ain't as they were!" Joe picked them up and handed them to Fred, who refused to take them.

"No! I want you to see!"

Fred could not look away or even close his eyes. It was as though he had no free will.

"That's right," Joe said. "You have to look!"

There, before him, Joe held two little dolls, beautifully fashioned with perfect features. Yet their smiles were fixed and their eyes looked frightened.

"This is monstrous. You lunatic!"

Joe sighed. "You worry too much. I'll take care of it. They'll be able to speak and move around. Right now they can't because the change has to come slowly."

Joe pointed to their bodies. They looked like a man and woman. Joe touched Al's tiny penis. "Look at that. It can't be erect now but it will be. They'll be able to do everything they could do before the change."

The Darla doll fell over and Joe said he thought she was upset. So he picked her up and stared at her smiling. "So perfect. Amazing, isn't it?"

His expression turned serious then. "See, when the magic is finished and they can speak and are fully demonized, they will be like the dolls in the stand you ran with Hank. It's going to be interesting to see who they go to."

Suddenly, the Darla doll hissed.

Joe laughed. "Oh, she's pissed off. Ain't you, honey, but you'll be alright. Uncle Joe will look after you." He winked and popped her into his pocket for special attention later, he said. He made a waving motion and Fred saw the dolls from the stand. "They were made from my enemies, Fred. Take a look!"

Sure enough, Fred saw the soldier doll turn into a man. "That's how he had looked. He tried to harm me when I carried his fiancée off. So I made sure they'd always be together. And here, look at these. Pretty exotic, huh?"

Fred looked to see an assortment of dolls, one of which was a toy monkey playing a drum.

Joe grinned. "Now, he's a favorite of mine, the initial experiment. He was never a real monkey. Just a man from another place."

The monkey started to scream. "Yup." Joe shook his head. "Still pissed off. He didn't want to be summoned from Hell, but he was. He's used to it now though. I fashioned him and other small demons into toys. Very popular they are, too. They possess folk, that's their purpose, see? The rest are different." Joe gestured toward the other dolls. "These were the sideshow stars that left. They got a little too big for their britches. The fat lady was a bitch on wheels. She took a knife to me once!"

Fred looked and to his horror, he realized the doll had been mutilated.

"See? I cut off her arms and legs and breasts, too. Then I realized that was stupid. Who's gonna buy a doll like that? Anyhow, I leave her alone. She's in another place. Doesn't know where she is kind of thing." He nodded and pointed out the rest of his former sideshow. "Yup, they brought it on themselves by disobeying and not respecting me. And the religious ones! Man! Was that a pain in the ass... Better not tell you where they wound up!"

Fred couldn't take anymore, but Joe just continued: "It's not as hard as you think. Just a few well-placed words and this soldier doll for example becomes just a toy for kids to play with! Now, his girl..." Joe smiled. "See, look here..." He held up a beautiful little woman doll. "I keep her around for my personal entertainment. She's too good for the stand. Don't want her bought, see?"

The little doll screamed but Joe only laughed.

Fred didn't pay that much mind because he was screaming, too.

\* \* \*

Joe looked thoughtful. "That's right, you let it out. Better out than in. Now then—where was I? Oh yes! The clowns."

Happy, the demon, was devouring something bloody.

"See, they were already half-way there anyway. It was nothing to make them fully fledged demons. Now they'll work out of Hell and the circus. Can't wait to see what they get up to. See their wings? Oh yes, that's right! They are fully demonized now!"

Noble and Danny flew over to Fred. They were no longer scarred. "We'll still wear our clown makeup though," Noble said. Each had bloody, gore-encrusted mouths from feeding on the stomped children and their parents.

"Love you, fellas. You will serve just fine!"

Hank called out to Joe. "What about me, Joe? Ain't you going to tell me what my surprise is?"

Joe slapped his leg. "Sure! Nearly forgot, kid. You get to stay in Hell forever!"

Hank turned white and sank to his knees. "But I served faithfully. I was to be one of the chosen. You promised!"

"The way it goes, kid. It's your fate. You won't find loyalty here, or honesty for that matter. Not here!"

Fred cried out as scores of winged demons flew down to attack Hank.

"Don't worry," Joe said. "He'll get used to it. Not that he has any choice."

Hank's screams were horrific.

"This isn't even Hell yet." Joe laughed. "What's he going to do when we get there?"

# Chapter 39

Hank was still screaming when the gondola moved again.

"Okay, this is it," Joe said. "Just you, your pa, and me now. Prepare yourselves, this is the roughest bit. I give you Hell, gentlemen!"

There were two more doors, with demons on either side—tall, winged beings, not covered with scales, though. In fact, they looked like minotaurs from Greek legend, half man, half bull.

Fred could feel the heat even before the doors were opened, and from his face, so did Old Pa.

"It's pretty hot," Joe said. "Better cover your faces!"

They tried to but the door opened quickly and the smell of their flesh burning permeated the air. They cried out. Fred started to shout obscenities, but Joe just laughed as usual.

"Now it's different. You are burning but it won't kill you, you're past that. As hard as it may be to believe, you will get used to it."

Fred protested, but as the heat worsened, he fell silent. Old Pa clung to him, crying. If Fred had any rational thoughts at all, they were of a remorseful nature. Both had killed. He was as bad as his father, just as evil, perhaps worse. He knew that now.

If only... he thought. Ah but it was far too late for *if onlies*. Regret mattered not. Hell might as well have a sign posted above the doors: LEAVE REGRET OUTSIDE. IT HAS NO PLACE IN HELL.

Fred's mind started to wander. Maybe it wasn't real; maybe it was a nightmare.

A voice screamed in his ear.

NO, THIS IS REAL LIKE THAT SUCCUBUS GETTING YOU OFF, REMEMBER THAT?

Fred looked down and saw the same longhaired creature. She was doing it again! Was there pleasure in Hell?

The sucking stopped and the creature looked up but rather than Dorinda, the beautiful succubus, this was an old hag, who cackled and started doing it all over again. Fred pulled at her hair to make her stop, but she kept on and as she did, she started to bite him. Little bites at first but then, she started to really chew.

Joe pushed her aside. Fred rubbed himself. "That's the Whore of Babylon, that is. Not really, kid," Joe said after a pause. "Don't believe everything you hear in Hell."

Joe let him wail a bit. When he was finished, he spoke again, "Look upon my truth! I have been many things in my existence!" He began to change then into a variety of hellish beasts and monsters. He stopped when he saw Fred wasn't watching.

"Won't bother without an audience. I always liked an audience. Now we come to the bridge."

There was indeed a bridge just ahead.

Joe helped them both out of the gondola. As soon as he did, the boat vanished. "There, look there." He pointed ahead. Fred didn't want to look but he did. The Lake of Fire.

He cried out for before him stretched a terrible, vast inferno of molten lava; only there were people in it, burning and screaming in agony.

"Sad, isn't it? Those are just some of the damned. There are more and they're not in the Lake," Joe said, gesturing upward. "See them levels and shelves? The damned dwell there, different levels for different sins—some poet wrote about it once. The thing was, Satan didn't let him in. He showed him some bullshit and the poor slob goes away thinking he saw Hell but he never did! He only saw what Satan wanted him to see. Don't ask me why. I just work here."

Joe went on to say he had been with Satan from the beginning, that he was one of the very first recruits. "Yeah, I've always been here it seems. And you know what I think? I think it was a shit thing that happened to him. Satan was alright, kind of stuck on himself though, you might say. So big deal." Joe shrugged. "Now, I'm going to show you the levels. Come. Hold on tight to me. We can fly up, see? Just don't let go or you'll be fucked."

Fucked and burning in the Lake of Fire.

"The top level is for assholes mainly, jerkoffs, thieves, rapists, child molesters. Let me show you."

They met them. Most of them were men from every walk of life. Teachers and parsons, men who shouted their confessions:

"*I used my position to abuse those given over to my care.*"

"*I sinned and will burn in Hell!*"

"*I raped my wife's sister. I said she asked for it but I lied.*"

"Bob's there, remember Bob? Look."

Bob looked to be praying. "I have sinned. I deserve to burn…"

Joe waved him off. "He's a ham. Shoulda been an actor."

Bob was just one of many of the damned shouting their confessions. On it went and with each and every confession, Joe shook his head. "You have no one to blame but yourselves!".

They agreed though they screamed in agony.

There were nine levels in all. Joe said that poet, Dante, was told there were nine circles of Hell and that number was right—but that was the only piece of correct information he'd received. The other levels were crowded with whores and arsonists, murderers and hypocrites, equally distributed.

Joe said he figured Hell had more hypocrites than anything else. "These here are the political leaders that Heaven won't take. They not only won't take them, they insist we house them. There are all kinds here, including senators from ancient times and modern times. If you look around, you'll recognize a few and some heads of state, presidents, kings and queens, and crazy motherfuckers like evil conquerors and emperors. We got them all!"

"Where will we be? Which level?"
Joe scratched his chin. "That, son, is as yet undecided."

\* \* \*

They were finished, fucked, and they knew it. Both of them did, even Old Pa. This place—what with its damned burning and the Lake of Fire—sharpened their wits. It focused their brains. Joe said it did and it was true.

"You're all the same, you people. You always were. Some are worse than others. But I always know. I can tell where there's fertile ground and where there isn't. I know what the harvest will offer, who's on my side and who never can be. But the most ironical thing is," Joe said with a smile, "those who are damned don't realize it until it's too late."

Fred pleaded again, but in vain.

"Look Fred. You're here because of what you did. Both of you. Understand?"

He did, really. There was no more fear, just acceptance—that and suffering. "I'm ready," he said, knowing he would never see Andy because he was not going to be in Hell. "Andy…"

Joe grinned. "Devout. Couldn't catch him out. Not an angel but no devil either… whereas you…"

"Just get on with it! Cut the crap!" Fred yelled.

Joe looked pleased. "I knew you'd understand… Some folks take longer than others."

He was truly resigned. There was nothing else to do. No pleading or escaping. This was it.

"Watch the Lake. That's his favorite place," Joe said, and they did.

There, in the very center of it, Satan emerged in all his horrific glory—with his great wings and horns. Up he went like the Kraken of legend, so large he filled the central portion of the chamber. The damned cried out in fear and horror. It was as Joe had said—"If hate never dies, neither does fear—'specially here!"

Fred sank to his knees for the sight was so fantastic, so amazing. He bowed his head in supplication. "I am ready to burn," he wept.

Joe touched his head in a fatherly fashion. "I can help you, my son. You don't have to burn. You just have to throw your father into the fire. That's all you have to do. How about it?"

He did it without hesitation. He did it without guilt or sorrow. He just picked up that fucking old bag of bones that was his father and tossed him away without feeling anything.

His father screamed all the way down and when his body hit the fiery liquid, Fred didn't give a shit.

"The sell-out. Never fails. Now is your judgment," Joe said and he picked Fred up. "You will dwell with those who have harmed their parents. If throwing your father into the Lake of Fire isn't harming... what is?"

Fred was betrayed. As he knew himself, he had been well and truly fucked. Tricked most cruelly, but there was no reason to argue. He'd burn forever, along with all the other damned. His fate was sealed. There was nothing after this, not ever.

*It will always be like this...there is no escape.*

Thus he became another occupant of Hell. The heat felt far more intense and he cried out. The last thing he heard before the burning started was Joe's voice inside his head: HELL CAN BITE YOU IN THE ASS, BOY—DON'T YOU KNOW THAT? AIN'T NO LOGIC IN HELL!

# Epilogue

*The man was well dressed. He liked Joe, said he was amused by him. "I've always liked show people and as for circus people, that is a double treat for me. This is most interesting. I am entranced!"*

*Joe was never more ingratiating. He stared at his new friend with such devotion, it was almost embarrassing. The man began to squirm so Joe toned himself down.*

*"Yes," the man said. I think you and your employees will find everything most suitable. It is a new ship—and quite well-fitted out. You will be most comfortable in third class. Third class on one of my vessels is like second class on most others." He paused a moment. "Tell me again about your circus. I have always loved such things since I was a child."*

*Joe was delighted. But so was his listener. He wanted to hear more, not only about the clowns but about the acrobats as well. "That is something that has always fascinated me. They are not only skilled, they are fearless."*

*Joe agreed.*

*Then it got down to money. Joe bravely began to speak of it. "We can entertain the passengers to make up the difference—if you would permit us to do so. Putting on little skits to charm them at meal time or afterwards, perhaps in the lounge..."*

*"That would be charming. Yes, what a good idea! I tell you what," the man said. "Why don't you just consider yourselves workers, performers*

on the ship? You will be put up in cabins—they are quite nice. The crew has no complaints."

Joe was incredulous. "You mean you don't wish any money to be paid for our passage...?"

"That is quite right! Not a penny! No, you are entertainers, are you not?"

"That is most kind of you," Joe said. "I can't wait to tell my people."

"Well," Herr Dossing said. "Tell them, by all means. Tell them that you sail from Baltimore to Hamburg on Thursday next—you know you will be in time for the Octoberfest! That is a great time in Germany!"

Joe smiled. "I am certain change is coming—great change, and all of it will be most exciting."

The two shook hands again.

Herr Dossing watched him leave; he felt very excited indeed. Circus people on one of his ships! How amazed the passengers would be. He was quite certain it would be very good for business. Yes, things were looking brighter!

\* \* \*

Joe couldn't wait. This was one of his favorite centuries. In fact, he thought it might just prove eventually to contain the most damned. Of course, he'd have to see. But there was no rush—he liked to take his time.

And really, it wasn't that difficult opening gateways. All he needed were some likely losers with a propensity for evil. Simplest thing in the world.

# Other Books by the Author

- The Blackstone Vampires
    - The House on Blackstone Moor
    - Unholy Testament – The Beginnings
    - Unholy Testament – Full Circle
    - The Fourth Bride
- Justine – Into the Blood
- House of Horrors

# Contents

Chapter 1 — 1

Chapter 2 — 5

Chapter 3 — 9

Chapter 4 — 13

Chapter 5 — 17

Chapter 6 — 21

Chapter 7 — 25

Chapter 8 — 31

Chapter 9 — 36

Chapter 10 — 41

Chapter 11 — 48

Chapter 12 — 53

Chapter 13 — 58

| | |
|---|---|
| Chapter 14 | 64 |
| Chapter 15 | 69 |
| Chapter 16 | 73 |
| Chapter 17 | 77 |
| Chapter 18 | 81 |
| Chapter 19 | 85 |
| Chapter 20 | 89 |
| Chapter 21 | 93 |
| Chapter 22 | 97 |
| Chapter 23 | 101 |
| Chapter 24 | 106 |
| Chapter 25 | 110 |
| Chapter 26 | 115 |
| Chapter 27 | 119 |
| Chapter 28 | 122 |
| Chapter 29 | 126 |
| Chapter 30 | 130 |
| Chapter 31 | 134 |
| Chapter 32 | 138 |

*Carole Gill*

| | |
|---|---|
| Chapter 33 | 143 |
| Chapter 34 | 147 |
| Chapter 35 | 153 |
| Chapter 36 | 158 |
| Chapter 37 | 164 |
| Chapter 38 | 168 |
| Chapter 39 | 174 |
| Epilogue | 179 |